RENEGADE

TIN STAR K9 SERIES - BOOK 1

JODI BURNETT

DEDICATION

For my Family
To Trevor, Emily, Skyler, and Sarah who taught me what crazy,
fierce, overwhelming, and unconditional love feels like. That's how
I love the four of you. You're my very best.

1

The inky blackness of the cool spring night soothed Caitlyn's frustration. Relief at having somewhere else to go reaffirmed her decision to move out. The fact that her brother, Dylan, would probably never forgive her was his problem. She absently stroked the furry head resting in her lap as she drove down the forest highway toward Moose Creek. Renegade, her German Shepherd-Malinois mix, slept stretched over the bench seat of her truck, using her leg as a pillow. Caitlyn and Renegade had been together for almost two years now, and she couldn't imagine her life without his company.

Wispy fog rose from the river fifty-feet below to her right, drifting across the highway, permeating the night with a spooky atmosphere. The winding mountain road worked against her like a hypnotist's watch, mesmerizing her toward sleep. She fisted her fingers and ground them into her dry and gritty eyes. Caitlyn cracked open her window to get some fresh air, then reached over Renegade to change the radio station to something more upbeat.

She'd barely glanced away from the road, but when she

I

looked up again, high-beam headlights glared into the cab, careening toward her from the black abyss on her left. Caitlyn's brain scrambled to make sense of the direction from which the impending collision came as she instinctively slammed on her brakes. The rear end of her truck fish-tailed and skidded toward the edge of the steep embankment that plunged to the river fifty feet below. One of her back wheels dropped off the soft shoulder, causing a sudden jerk that threw Renegade into the dashboard. He yelped and fell onto the floorboard.

One second before impact, tires screeched and the car racing toward her swerved, barely missing a direct broadside crash, though still clipping her front end. The sick sound of crumpling metal echoed through the cab, and her truck lurched perilously toward the cliff's edge. Caitlyn stood on her brakes, praying her backend wouldn't slide off, tumbling hood over tailgate to the bottom of the ravine. Never slowing, the smaller vehicle sped away into the night, leaving them to their fate.

Caitlyn flipped her pickup into four-wheel drive and sucking in a deep breath, braved shifting her foot from brake to gas. In that heartbeat, the truck bed dropped as the second tire skidded over the edge. She floored the gas, the engine roared, and rocky gravel riddled the underside of her rig.

With a growling surge, the truck fought the battle against gravity until Caitlyn barreled onto solid ground. Once safely on the pavement, she jammed the pickup into park. "Ren? Are you okay?"

Her dog climbed onto the seat and licked her face. Caitlyn hugged him tight and held on, trembling as her pulse steadied and the adrenaline flooding her system receded. She turned the cab light on to check on Renegade. Her hands ran over his bones and belly, searching for lumps and bruises until she was confident he wasn't injured. "Where the hell did that car come from?" Ren answered with another long swipe of his tongue. "That idiot could have killed us!"

Caitlyn rummaged in the glove box for her flashlight. She clicked on her hazard lights and opened her door. It was too dark to see skid marks on the pavement, but the lingering smell of burning rubber assured her they were there. She and Renegade crossed the barren highway. Caitlyn flashed her beam into the foliage on the mountainside of the street. Her light panned across a rugged, forest-service entry road. "It was probably just some kids who were up on the mountain drinking and hooking up." She shivered at the knowledge of how close they'd come to slipping off the highway and tumbling down the rocky cliff to the rushing waters below.

Having made sense of where the car came from, Caitlyn and her dog returned to the truck. She shined the light on the dented front bumper. The car smashed her signal light too, but it could have been a lot worse. She opened the door and told Renegade to load up. Once inside, she locked the doors and sat back against her seat, still shaking from the experience. Caitlyn considered calling the sheriff, but there was nothing to tell. Yes, it was a hit and run, but she had only seen headlights and taillights. She couldn't describe the vehicle at all. And besides, this late at night she'd end up having to talk to Colt, and that was something she wanted to avoid at all costs.

2
———

On Sunday morning, Caitlyn bumped along the gravel road that wound through a thick pine forest and led to her family's ranch. Renegade sat next to her on the front seat, his tongue lolling out the side of his mouth. The Reed Ranch had been in her family since the 1800s and was as familiar to her as her most comfortable pair of boots. Caitlyn had always loved this drive. It meant she was coming home. However, she reminded herself, her recent decision meant that was no longer the case. She wanted to move toward her future, even if she had no idea what that future was.

Caitlyn shrugged off the uncomfortable edginess that poked the underside of her ribs. Ignoring the constant pall from her lack of personal direction, she rolled down the window of her silver truck. Her parents had given her the used vehicle when she went off to college—the second time. Brisk pine-infused air freshened the warm, muggy cab, bringing with it a resolve to find her path. But first, she wanted to fix things with her brother. Caitlyn took a deep breath and let it bolster the confidence she needed to face him.

Friday night, Dylan had been furious—as usual—and forgiveness looked as far away as ever. Caitlyn understood his anger, but wished that he would consider her point of view, too. She hoped he'd let her explain herself today. She reached for the thermal mug nestled in the cup-holder and pulled in a long sip of her strong black coffee. The stout brew buoyed her determination as she maneuvered around the twists and turns through the woods on the way to her family's log-cabin home.

The sun was up enough to warm the eastern logs of the house by the time she drove past the driveway and continued down to the barnyard beyond. Dylan was already out and hard at work, his breath puffing like a cigar in the cool morning air. Caitlyn parked beside Dylan's mount, hitched to a rail next to the arena gate. She raised her hand in greeting to her brother, who was bent over, holding up one of his horse's feet. He pounded a nail through the iron shoe and out the side wall of the hoof, then deftly clipped the sharp point off. He barely gave Caitlyn a quick nod in response.

"Good morning." Caitlyn schooled her features to disguise the apprehension she felt. She was tired of his scowl and perpetual surly attitude, when all she wanted was to smooth things out. She pressed on, "Did Sampson throw a shoe?"

"Nope." Dylan's simmering anger percolated under the tone of his one-word answer.

Caitlyn turned off her engine and unclipped her seatbelt. She rested her chin on her arms in the open window. "Just tightening things up?" Dylan responded with a glower at her rhetorical question. The beard he'd grown for winter did nothing to hide his expression, and his dark eyes, the same shade of mahogany as hers, sparked with irritation.

Caitlyn sighed and opened her door. She hopped down to the ground from her seat. Renegade followed her out, his red-tawny fur glowing in the sunrise. "What can I help you with this morning?" She grabbed her straw cowboy hat from the truck and settled it on her head. Her long, dark-brown hair hung in a single thick braid down her back.

"What are you doing here? This isn't your ranch anymore, remember?" Dylan placed the hoof-nail hammer in a slot on his shoeing stand before moving it out of his way. He smoothed a rough hand down his horse's neck and reached to check the saddle cinch. He kept his broad back to Caitlyn as he tightened it.

"Come on, Dylan. Aren't you tired of this same old argument? This will always be our family's ranch, and I'm a part of that." Caitlyn patted Sampson's haunches. "I'm more than happy to do my share of the work. I just don't want to live here anymore."

"You've made that crystal clear. Don't you have chores you should be doing at your own place?" Dylan exchanged Sampson's halter with a bridle, sliding the bit carefully into his horse's mouth.

Caitlyn clamped down on a defensive retort. She swallowed. "Where are you riding to?"

"Checking on the cows."

"Want me to saddle up and come out with you? Or is there something else you need done?" Caitlyn crossed her arms over her chest.

Dylan yanked his leather work gloves on and gathered his reins to the horn. He climbed into the saddle and turned his horse to face her. "I'm sure you can find something to do while I'm gone." With that, he spun Sampson around and urged him into a lope down the path towards the distant cattle pastures.

Caitlyn sighed. "Well, Ren, there are always stalls to clean. Let's get to work." She stepped off toward the big red barn. Her boots crunched the gravel, and Renegade kept pace beside her. Pausing inside the door for her eyes to adjust to the dimness, Caitlyn inhaled the familiar and comforting blend of wood shavings, horse sweat, leather, and manure. Whiskey, her bay gelding, knickered at her as she entered, and his welcome made her smile. Caitlyn was saving to build a shelter and corral at her new property so she could bring her horse home. Until then, Whiskey would have to bunk here.

Caitlyn approached his stall, and her horse poked his head out of the opening to greet her. She ran her fingers over his broad cheek and scratched behind his black ear. He stretched his neck farther over the stall door and sniffed at Renegade. Their noses touched, and Whiskey twitched his velvet lips. Caitlyn noted Dylan had already fed the horses, so she went to find a rake and wheelbarrow. Eight stalls later, and as many trips to the manure pile, Caitlyn finished mucking. She was guzzling a cold drink from the hose when Dylan returned.

"You're still here?" Dylan swung his leg over the saddle and jumped down. He tethered Sampson to the hitching post, and with his hands on his hips, he turned to glare at Caitlyn. His favorite black cowboy hat lent shade to his already dark expression.

"I just finished cleaning out the stalls for you." Caitlyn pressed the red lever of the water spigot down to shut it off.

"For *me*? I thought you said this was still the *family* ranch. Make up your mind, Caitlyn. You can't have it both ways."

"You know what I mean, Dylan. When are you gonna let this go? I'm getting really sick of this pettiness."

"You're welcome to leave anytime." Dylan's expression matched his harsh tone, and he took a step toward her. Renegade moved between them and growled at him. "You better get control of your dog if you know what's good for him."

"Now you're threatening my dog? How do you think Logan would feel about that?" She knew that would push a button. Her brothers were close, and Dylan had nothing but love and respect for his younger brother. She wished Dylan felt the same way toward her.

"Don't drag Logan into this. He doesn't live here either."

"That's true, but you don't seem to hold that against *him*."

"Logan didn't sell out." Dylan struck off toward the barn.

"Please, don't walk away. Are you refusing to talk to me about why you're so angry because you're afraid?" Caitlyn jogged after him.

"I'm not afraid of anything."

"I think maybe you're scared to fail on your own, and you're pissed that I put you in that position."

Dylan spun around to face her. "Caitlyn, it's time for you to leave my ranch. I'm not afraid, I just don't have time to deal with this crap. You don't want to live here, so go home." Her brother clenched his fists and his jaw twitched.

His rage didn't frighten her, though. "I can't believe you." Caitlyn's voice rose with matching anger. The burnt-orange fur on Renegade's top-line and shoulders bristled and his menacing growl rolled into a snarl.

Chickens clucked and scurried in Caitlyn's peripheral view, and their mother rushed out of the chicken pen, hurrying toward them. The woven gardening hat she wore flew off her thick silver-streaked hair on her way. "Will you two please stop fighting like children?"

"I came here this morning to patch things up, Mom, but Dylan is too pig-headed and stubborn to let me."

"He just needs some time, Catie." She handed Caitlyn a

full basket of eggs and resettled her hat. "Why don't you come inside for a cup of coffee?"

"Time?" Caitlyn accepted the load. "He's been mad at me since last fall." Her frustration reached a boiling point, and she kicked the dirt. "I have just as much right to be here as Dylan does."

"What right do you have?" Dylan bellowed. "You sold your right, try to remember that. And now, I have to break my back every day because of it."

Caitlyn stuck her tongue out at her brother and instantly felt like an immature idiot. If their argument had seemed childish to her mother before, Caitlyn confirmed it. Dylan was the one person who could frustrate her into behaving like a kid.

Their mom regarded Dylan with a level blue-gray gaze until he relaxed his fists, then she turned her disapproving expression to Caitlyn. "I think you need to let your brother be for a little while. Let him cool off." She hooked her arm through Caitlyn's and pulled her toward the house. "I heard something interesting on the news this morning. Do you remember Wendy Gessler? You went to school with her, didn't you?"

Caitlyn knew Wendy. They had been good friends in junior high, though they hadn't hung around with each other much in high school. Wendy had gone boy-crazy, while Caitlyn was still in love with her horses. "Yeah, why? What did she do to get on the news?"

Metal clanged behind them, and Caitlyn glanced back to see Dylan hauling several fencing tools out to his horse. "Hey Dylan, you remember Wendy Gessler, don't you?" He flashed her a glare. "You two dated, didn't you?"

"What of it?"

Their mom cocked her head at him. "I don't remember that."

"It was just a couple of times, Ma. No reason you'd know."

"Either way, I heard on the news this morning that she's gone missing." Dylan's hands stilled, then both he and Caitlyn looked at their mother. "Apparently, she never came home on Friday night, and no one has seen her since then. Her family is terribly worried."

"That's weird. Doesn't she teach at the middle school?" Caitlyn glanced at Dylan to see if he knew.

He nodded. "Last I heard, she taught eighth-grade history."

"That's what they said on the news." Their mother walked back towards Dylan, and Caitlyn followed. "Have you kept in touch with her?"

"Not really. Not more than to say hello if I see her in town or at the Mercantile." Dylan attached the fencing tools to his saddle with Concho straps. "I'm sure she'll turn up." He pulled himself onto Sampson's back.

Caitlyn agreed. "I bet she shows up for work at the school tomorrow morning."

"I've got stuff to do." Dylan acknowledged his mother with the tip of his hat but ignored Caitlyn.

"Wait, Dylan." Caitlyn reached out as though she could stop him. "Where are you going to be? I'll saddle up, meet you out there, and give you a hand." Caitlyn passed the basket of eggs back to her mother.

"What about that cup of coffee?" Caitlyn's mom touched her shoulder.

"That's right, Caitlyn. You're a guest on this ranch, and Mom treats guests to coffee and muffins." Dylan nudged his horse and trotted away toward the northern pasture.

"Thanks, Mom, but I'm gonna help Dylan with that fence whether he likes it or not. I want to work this thing out between us. I hate that he's still so mad at me, and I'm tired of him treating me like crap. I know he's angry, but I don't deserve that."

"Well, you must admit your decision put a big financial strain on him, and on this ranch. At least try to understand why he's so upset."

Caitlyn pushed her cowboy hat firmly down on her head. "Oh, I understand why he's angry. But he has no say over my third of our inheritance, or what I do with it."

"Yes, my dear, but your decisions affected him directly. Part of why he's angry is because he didn't have any say in a decision that changed his life." Caitlyn's mom sighed and then, squeezing her arm, moved to a different subject. "Will you be here for dinner?"

"Sure." Caitlyn peeked at her mother from under the brim of her hat and grinned. "If Dylan doesn't kill me first. Promise me, if I don't show up for dinner, you'll send someone out to look for my body in the northern pasture."

Her mom pursed her lips and shook her head. She turned toward the ranch house toting her basket of eggs. "I'll see you tonight, honey."

Caitlyn waved goodbye to her mom. On their way to the barn, Renegade spotted a rabbit and darted off on the hunt. She loved to watch him run. With his fox-colored topcoat and black-as-pitch face, legs, and underbelly—he was strikingly beautiful. Caitlyn's thoughts drifted to her brother Logan, who was an FBI K-9 handler in Denver. He had taught her everything she knew about training dogs, and he wouldn't approve of her allowing Renegade to run free as much as she did. Her dog was well-behaved, but he wasn't a trained police dog. He was more of a ranch dog—one who liked to chase rabbits.

Caitlyn pushed open the stall door and slid a halter over Whiskey's head. "Come on, boy. Time to go to work." She tied him to the hitching post and returned to the barn for his tack. When she had saddled him and they were ready to go, Caitlyn whistled for Renegade, and her dog sprinted to her side. They followed the path through the tall grasses that Dylan had taken on his way to mend fences. She'd ridden about three miles when she saw the sun glinting off the fence-stretcher that Dylan was working with. She loped over to meet him.

Without looking at her, he grumbled, "What do you want now?" Dylan peered up at her and wiped his forehead with the back of his forearm.

"You know, Dylan, this ranch will fully belong to you one day—not me, or Logan. Aren't you happy about that? You love this place. I just needed my share now so I could get started on living my life."

Dylan clamped the wire stretching tool onto a broken end of barbed wire. "Then, go live your life."

"Look, just because I want a place of my own, doesn't mean I don't care about you and the ranch."

"Let me see if I've got this straight. You want your own place, you supposedly want independence, but you want to work here, keep your horse here, and get fed here. What kind of independence is that? You don't even have a job." He clamped the other side of the broken wire onto the tool and ratcheted the strands toward each other.

"I do too. I've been taking some shifts at the café." Caitlyn defended herself, but Dylan was right. She was at loose ends, not sure what she wanted to do with her life. She was thankful her dad understood her need to be out on her own and believed she'd eventually find her vocation. "I'm off today, so I thought maybe you could use my help. And I'm saving up to build a shelter and corral for Whiskey." She reached forward and patted her horse's powerful neck. "Then I'll take him off your hands. Until then, Dad said I could keep him here."

Dylan glared up at her again, holding her gaze for an uncomfortably long moment. "Dad's always let you get away with murder." He stepped away from the fence. "If you really want to help, ride back to the barn, load a spool of barbed wire into the ATV wagon, and bring it out here. Looks like I'm going to need to restring a good part of this fence."

Caitlyn sensed a whisper of an olive branch in his words. Their disagreement was far from over, but maybe Dylan was ready to take a step forward. "Sure thing. We'll be right back." Caitlyn turned her horse and called out, "Come on, Ren. Let's go." She loped to the barn, gratified her brother was willing to let her stay and help, at least for a little while.

3

Caitlyn and Dylan worked together side-by-side, mostly in silence, throughout the day. They restrung the fence and patched several other areas the cows had busted through. Back at the ranch house after work, Caitlyn washed up for supper. She thought about her time with Dylan. He hadn't said many words to her, but his attitude seemed to soften. *Hopefully dinner will go well too. Maybe I can draw him into a regular conversation.* Caitlyn dried her face and hands on a fluffy white towel, then she and Renegade rumbled down the back stairs to the kitchen to see if her mother needed any help. Cooking was not her forte. In fact, most household chores were a challenge for Caitlyn. She much preferred the hard, physical work of a ranch.

"Is there anything I can do, Mom?" She approached her mother from behind and rested her hands on the woman's soft shoulders. She kissed her mom's cheek and peered down at the magic happening in the pot on the stove.

"For one thing, you can get that dog out of my kitchen. Dinner is just about ready. Why don't you carry the salad in and fill the water glasses?" Her mom stirred something bubbly that smelled savory and delightful, causing Caitlyn's stomach to roll in anticipation.

She swept the salad bowl off the counter and made her way to the dining room. "Come on, Ren. Your fur is not welcome in Mom's lair."

Caitlyn's dad and Dylan stood together before a blazing fire in the massive stone fireplace of the great-room. A seven-point elk's head mount stood guard from the rock chimney above them. Both men held stout tumblers of bourbon. The two men bore a strong resemblance, but Dylan's frame was thicker. Logan was the one who looked most like their dad, with his leaner build and finer features. The only real differences between those two were the graying at her father's temples and the weathered creases on his tanned face that spoke of a life lived on the range.

When her dad saw her enter the room, his obsidian eyes glimmered. He held his arm open for her to enter his embrace. Dylan, on the other hand, turned away from her. *Or maybe he is just warming his hands with the flames. Stop jumping to conclusions.* "You guys about ready for dinner?" Caitlyn set down the dish and went to hug her father.

"Hi Catie. I'm glad you're staying for supper."

"Thanks, Dad." Caitlyn's gaze moved to her brother. His stiff back implied he didn't share his father's sentiment.

Her Dad sipped his drink, and the ice reflected the amber flames. "Hey, I noticed the front quarter-panel on your truck is dented, and your turn light is broken."

"Yeah. Some drunk kids swerved into me after I left here the other night."

"Are you all right? Did you call the sheriff?"

Caitlyn's lungs compressed as she thought about how close she'd come to slipping off the cliff, but there was no need to worry her dad. "I'm fine. I probably should have called it in, but all I saw were lights. I couldn't describe the car, and it was late."

"You need to get that signal light fixed right away."

"I will." Caitlyn smiled at her dad. "Dylan, will you fill the water glasses?"

Dylan's shoulders slumped slightly. He tossed a glance over his shoulder at her. "I'm having a drink with Dad right now."

"No problem." Caitlyn chewed on her lower lip. *Are we back at square one, even after we had such a good day?* She told Renegade to stay and went into the kitchen to fill a pitcher with water. "What are Dad and Dylan in such a deep conversation about?"

"Nothing particular that I'm aware of." Her mother handed her a bowl of mashed potatoes. "Take these to the table, please. I think we're about ready. Tell the boys to come to dinner."

After their dad said grace, and they passed the serving dishes around, their mom brought up the local drama. "Has anyone heard more news about Wendy Gessler?"

Her dad sliced through a piece of meat, but before he bit into it, he answered, "Nothing new on the 5 o'clock news. Maybe the 6 o'clock broadcast will have something."

Dylan wiped his mouth on his napkin. "Why are they making such a big deal out of Wendy not coming home over the weekend? She never struck me as the super responsible type. She probably just drove down to Cheyenne for a couple of days and hasn't made it back yet."

"But no one can reach her." Their mom poured gravy over her mashed potatoes.

Caitlyn checked her watch. "The 6 o'clock news is in ten minutes. Do you mind if we turn it on, Mama?"

"You know I don't like the TV on during dinner." Her

mom pursed her lips. "But maybe this once. I'm curious too. I hope she's all right."

"I'm sure they'll find her soon." Caitlyn pushed her chair back and stood. "Most missing person cases end up being a miscommunication." She found the remote on the coffee table and clicked on the TV in the living room.

"Did you learn that in college?" Dylan said derisively.

"In fact, I did." Caitlyn gave him a bright smile, refusing to rise to his bait. She changed the channel to the local news station and bent to scratch Renegade's soft belly before she returned to her meal. The family waited for the program to come on, and at 6 o'clock, the broadcast banner flashed across the screen. The familiar ditty announcing the evening news played over the air. "Our headline story tonight is the missing person case of Wendy Gessler." The screen switched to the local field reporter, who asked Sheriff Tackett to share the case details.

At six foot, three-inches, the barrel-chested sheriff towered over the reporter as he peered into the camera. "Wendy Gessler is still missing. She was last seen on Friday night at the Tipsy Cow. We have interviewed almost everyone who was at the bar last Friday, her neighbors at the Pinewood apartment complex, and all of her coworkers. No one has seen or heard from her since Friday night. If anyone watching this newscast knows where Wendy is, or has heard from her, please call the Sheriff's Department immediately." A recent photo of the pretty blonde woman appeared on the screen. "Now, the family would like to make a few comments."

The young field reporter carried the oversized microphone to the family huddled together in a small group. Caitlyn recognized Mr. and Mrs. Gessler, but the thirty-something man who took the mic in his meaty hand was unfamiliar to her. His muscled shoulders rounded as he lowered his head of close-cropped dark hair. When he wiped at his eyes, Caitlyn noticed the tip of a tattoo edging out of his sleeve. He gathered himself and focused on the camera with slate-colored eyes.

"Wendy, if you're out there, and can hear us, please come home. We are worried about you. We miss you." Behind him, Wendy's mother and father stood in stoic silence, appearing overwhelmed with worry. The man shrugged against his suit-coat as though it didn't fit well and adjusted the microphone.

He continued. "If anyone knows anything about where Wendy is, or if you have seen her in the last couple of days, please, please, call the Sheriff's Office. Wendy, if you can hear me, I won't stop looking for you. Hold on, baby. I'm coming." The man released the mic to cover a sob with his palm, and the interviewer had to scramble to catch the device before it fell to the ground. Thick hands covered the man's face, and his shoulders shook.

"That guy must be Wendy's boyfriend," Caitlyn mused.

The camera focused on the reporter. "That was Mr. Jim Hague, Wendy Gessler's boyfriend, speaking for the family." He pointed out the phone number posted across the bottom of the screen to call with any information. Then the reporter turned the broadcast back to the anchor, who murmured her sympathies before deftly moving on to the next topic in the news.

"Dylan, do you know who that guy is? The boyfriend? I don't think I've seen him in Moose Creek before." Caitlyn took a bite of crisp salad soaked in tangy bleu cheese dressing.

Dylan scratched his chin. "I might've seen him at the bar. But I don't know who he is. Maybe he's new around here."

Caitlyn clamped the corner of her bottom lip between her teeth. She hadn't seen Wendy in months, and she had never seen the boyfriend before. But that didn't mean anything. It struck her as strange that he was far more emotional than Wendy's parents, though. She would have thought Wendy's mother would be the one to break down. But who knew? Everyone responded differently to fear and grief. "Does anyone else think his response was a little dramatic?"

"There you go again." Dylan looked at her out of the corner of his eyes. "Determining people's motivations for them."

"I'm not determining his motivation. Just wondering. His reaction seemed... overblown." Caitlyn glanced at her father, but he kept his face pointed toward his dinner plate. She shifted her eyes to her mom. "What do you think, Mom?"

"I don't know how I'd behave if you went missing, Caitlyn. But I know I'd be terribly upset." Her mom reached over and patted her hand.

"Maybe the Gesslers just don't want to display their feelings on the nightly news." Dylan leaned back in his chair.

Caitlyn knit her brows together and thought about that. "You're probably right, Dyl. But the boyfriend sure didn't seem to have any problem with it." Caitlyn finished her meal, chewing while she mulled over the newscast, her naturally inquisitive mind swirling with her observations. She wiped her mouth and set her napkin on her plate. "I wonder if they need volunteers to help search for her?"

"They didn't say anything about searching for her." Her mother reached for her husband's plate and stacked it on her own. "Do you think they'll put out a call?"

"Frankly, I'm surprised they haven't done so already. If for some reason Wendy was out in the woods lost, or hurt, it would be best to find her right away." Caitlyn held her hand out for Dylan's plate. He handed it to her with a little more force than necessary, but Caitlyn chose to ignore him. "I think I'll call the sheriff and see if they're starting a search party. Renegade is training to track, and this would be an excellent opportunity for him to practice at a live event."

Dylan draped his arm over the chair and leaned back. His eyes sparked with sarcasm. "I thought you said you wanted to help here at the ranch?"

"I did. I do want to help."

"We have a tourist trail ride scheduled for tomorrow, and well... I was hoping maybe you'd lead it for me?"

A rush of warmth spread through Caitlyn's chest, and a smile curled her lips. "I'd be happy to do that for you. Thanks, Dylan."

Dylan nodded, her mother clasped her hands together, and held them to her chin. Hope brimmed in her eyes.

"What time do you want me to be here?"

"We should start tacking up the horses around nine."

"Great!" This was the first concrete step Dylan had made toward reconciliation. Caitlyn wanted to take Renegade out and help search for Wendy, but she wasn't about to pass up the opportunity for healing her relationship with Dylan.

On her drive home, Renegade rested his chin in her lap, and Caitlyn stroked his head before dialing the Sheriff's Office. The phone rang three times before someone answered it. "Deputy Colt Branson here, how can I help you?"

Caitlyn's breath caught momentarily before she could find her words. For some reason, she hadn't expected Colt to answer the phone on a Sunday evening, and her heart gave a kick. "Colt? It's Caitlyn. Caitlyn Reed?"

There was a pause on the other end before Colt answered. "Hi Catie. How are you?"

"I'm fine. But I'm not calling about me. I was wondering if the sheriff is going to be running a search for Wendy Gessler? If so, I'd like to volunteer to help with my dog, Renegade."

"Oh, yeah. Isn't that the dog Logan helped you train?"

"Yes. I'm surprised you remembered." Caitlyn's pulse continued its jumpy acceleration.

He lowered his voice. "I remember everything."

Caitlyn wasn't sure what he meant by that, and she wasn't going to ask. They had a lot of history together, but it was all in the past. She hadn't seen Colt more than to wave at since she'd come home from college—the last time. "Okay, well, he's a trained tracker, and we'd be happy to help."

There was another long pause before Colt responded. "That's great. I'll let Sheriff Tackett know." He cleared his throat. "Listen, Catie, are you busy tomorrow afternoon? Want to meet me for a drink?"

Now it was Caitlyn's turn for a prolonged pause. She wasn't sure how she felt about Colt and was confused with how they had left things. "I'm running a trail ride in the morning for Dylan, and after that, I hope to be joining the search for Wendy."

"Maybe another time, then?" His voice dropped.

"Maybe." She needed time to think about their relationship, but she could only deal with one problem at a time. For now, Caitlyn wanted to focus on fixing things with Dylan. And tomorrow's trail ride was the first step.

"I'm going to keep asking, Catie, unless you tell me not to."

A rebellious grin pulled at Caitlyn's lips. "I'll see you later, Colt."

4

Caitlyn's alarm went off an hour earlier than usual, and she slapped at her phone screen to turn off the noise. It was still dark as she pulled on her clothes and filled Renegade's food and water dishes. She poured Lucky Charms into her own bowl and doused them with milk. She and her dog munched their breakfasts together—Caitlyn saving the sweet pastel marshmallows for last.

She hadn't led a trail ride up into the hills above their ranch since before she went away to college and was looking forward to it. The activities Caitlyn loved more than all others were spending time with Renegade and riding for hours on the back of her horse. If only she could make a living doing either of them, work would be a blast. Her usual sense of frustration washed over her as she thought about her future. She'd studied criminal justice at the University of Wyoming, but still didn't know what she wanted to do with her life.

Shaking off her pensiveness, Caitlyn drained the pinkish-green tinged milk and tossed her empty bowl into the sink. "Come on, Ren. We don't want to be late on our first day."

She grabbed a pack of beef jerky and a bottle of water before heading out the door. Forty-five minutes later, Caitlyn and Renegade pulled into the barnyard at Reed Ranch.

Dylan was in the arena and had already tacked up three of the six horses. Caitlyn opened the center console of her truck and removed her Glock 43 from its locked case. She snapped the magazine in place and clipped her gun into the thigh holster she used when riding in the backcountry. With Ren at her heels, she scurried from her truck. "Hey, why didn't you wait for me?"

Dylan avoided looking at her. "Work starts early on the ranch, remember?"

"The tourists won't be here for another two hours." Caitlyn didn't expect a response as she marched into the barn. She haltered more horses, leaving Whiskey for last. The graceful animals followed her out to the arena where she tied them and began the grooming process. Caitlyn brushed away the dust from their silky coats until they glistened in the sun. "My weather app says it's supposed to be a nice day."

"Good."

"What plans do you have for this morning? More fencing?"

"Getting the weaning pens ready. It's that time of year."

Caitlyn smiled to herself. Dylan had given her two full sentences without an attitude. That was progress. "I thought I'd take the riders to the top of the ridge, today. Maybe dip into the BLM on the far side. It's so beautiful up there."

Dylan's dark eyes flashed at her. "That might be too hard of a ride for newbies. Why don't you stay on the flatland? No need to risk going up on the mountain."

Caitlyn wasn't about to plod along on the boring flat prairie. "We'll see."

Ten minutes before their scheduled time, a minivan stuffed with five tourists parked outside the barn. They spilled out of the doors, wearing the bright colors and straw hats of vacationers. One man had a complex-looking camera hanging around his neck. Their loud joking was harsh against the peaceful morning as they took in their new surroundings. Dylan grumbled something under his breath and escaped to the tack room. On his way, he reached down and ruffled the fur on Renegade's head, causing Caitlyn to grin.

"Good morning, everyone." Caitlyn approached the new arrivals. "I'm Caitlyn Reed. I'll be leading you on your trail ride today." She shook each rider's hand and learned their names. "Do any of you have riding experience?"

One woman raised her thin arm. "I took English lessons as a girl. But that was a long time ago."

"Great! That's a start. And don't worry, we have specially selected horses that will take good care of you no matter what your skill level." Caitlyn assessed the group standing before her. She considered their sizes and assumed their athletic capabilities. As she assigned horses to riders, she heard Renegade's distinct growl.

She snapped her head around and saw Ren backed against the fence. His ears flat and turned back, a warning growl rumbled at the heavyset man who had bent to pet him. "Renegade, no! *Sedni*." The man drew his hand back, frowning. Caitlyn ran to her dog and knelt next to him.

"I'm sorry, sir. This is Renegade. I call him Ren, for short. He really is a good boy, but he's still young." She threw an arm around her dog's tense shoulders and felt his muscles relax. "I think he may have felt trapped against the fence. He's a rescue dog and needs more socialization." Her cheeks flared with heat as words tumbled across her tongue in embarrassment. Making the situation worse, Caitlyn glimpsed Dylan watching her from the shadow of the barn door with a scowl on his face.

The man who was the target of Renegade's warning backed away. "I don't feel safe around a dog who growls at me. He looked like he was going to bite me." The man turned to his friends. "I'm not sure we can trust the horses if we can't trust the dog. Should we rethink this? I don't want anyone getting hurt." The tourists furtively glanced at one another.

Dylan stepped out of the barn. "Good morning, folks. I'm Dylan Reed, Caitlyn's brother. Welcome to our ranch. I can guarantee that these horses are calm and well-trained. I hope you'll decide to stay and enjoy your ride." He tossed another scowl in Caitlyn's direction.

The man appeared unconvinced, shifting his weight from one foot to the other. "I don't know. What do you guys think?"

Before the others could answer, Caitlyn chimed in. "Dylan's right. I promise, these horses are perfectly safe." She stroked her dog's lean form. "Renegade is safe too. You probably just startled him. As I said, he's a rescue dog and needs to spend more time around people he doesn't know. Would you be willing to help me with that?" The man looked uncertain. "Try again. Let him smell your hand with me here next to him."

"Go on, Herb." A tall, slender woman urged. "You're always talking about how people should get their dogs from rescues. Now's your chance to practice what you preach."

The man scrunched his brows together and took a big breath. He gingerly reached his fingers forward. "Hello, Renegade. There's a good boy."

Caitlyn smoothed the fur between her dog's ears. "Good dog. It's okay, see?" She clasped the man's hand and shook it. Renegade watched every move. "Now it's your turn, boy." She nodded at Herb, who inched his hand closer to the dog. Renegade stretched his nose toward the man and sniffed.

Eventually, he licked the man's fingers and received an ear scratching for his good manners. Renegade wagged his tail, and the man laughed.

"You did it, Ren!" Caitlyn patted his head. "Thank you so much, Herb. This kind of socialization really helps him, and me."

"Happy to help. I love dogs, and good for you, for rescuing him." The man stood a little taller as Caitlyn introduced him to his horse. It relieved her that Renegade hadn't cost them the lucrative trail ride, or more importantly, the ground she'd made with her brother.

Caitlyn fitted her riders with helmets, and Dylan helped her get the guests mounted. She went over a few riding instructions and some basic trail safety points before she climbed on Whiskey and led the way out of the arena. "I'll stay in the lead. Be sure to maintain a horse's length between yourself and the horse in front of you. If you have any trouble or questions, don't hesitate to let me know. Keep your cameras ready—you're in for some panoramic views. Let's go." She reined her horse toward the path that led to the foothills and whistled for Renegade. "We'll be back here in time for lunch." She waved at Dylan as they rode away, and it shocked her when he returned the gesture. Probably just trying to make a good impression on the guests.

The group plodded through the flat grassy pasture on their way to the mountains. Caitlyn took her time, allowing the riders to settle into the movement of their horses and get used to their saddles. They passed the old tree swing she and her brothers used to play on. A white wooden cross stood planted under the tree now.

"Is that a family grave marker?" The tall woman rode up beside Caitlyn.

A whisper of sadness circled Caitlyn's heart, but she smiled. "No. That cross stands as a memorial to my brother

Logan's K9 partner he had in the Army. He was killed in an explosion in Afghanistan. His name was Lobo."

"Oh, I'm sorry."

"It's okay." She allowed the sudden wave of melancholy brought on by the memory to pass. "He was the same breed of dog as Renegade. It's one of the reasons I chose him."

Caitlyn halted the riders and stepped Whiskey out to the side so everyone could see her. "We'll be climbing up a mountain path that sometimes has tree roots or rocks the horses will have to navigate. Take your time and trust your horse. They know where to put their feet. Hold on to your saddle horn if you need to and be sure not to crowd each other on the trail."

When they got to the trailhead and took their first steps up the face of the mountain, a stiff wind spun a whirling dervish through their line, kicking dust up in their faces. Caitlyn shivered. In her experience, those mini-tornados often were dark portents of things to come.

5

The bracing pine scent invigorated Caitlyn, but she halted her horse. The breeze wrestled with the trees, keeping the riders comfortable in the sunshine, but it was still chilly in the shade. Though the trail was smooth at the beginning, Caitlyn turned in her saddle to make sure everyone was doing well as they started up the mountain. Renegade, who was running ahead on the trail, turned back and cocked his head, likely wondering why they had stopped.

"If you're cold, now would be a good time to put on your jackets. We'll mostly be in the shade on the way up." She waited as the riders struggled to untie their coats from around their waists and slip them on. Her gaze panned over the horses, and she grinned, pride welling in her chest. The animals stood steady, none of them moved while their riders adjusted their clothing. When everyone had settled in, Caitlyn waved her arm and pointed forward. "Ride on."

Soon, the incline steepened, and the horses had to step carefully over the natural obstacles on the trail. Renegade scampered first on one side of the route, and then the other.

Caitlyn stopped every two or three switchbacks to allow her guests to shoot photos of the breathtaking scenery from the hillside. It was still spring in northern Wyoming, and some spots on the path were muddy from the winter runoff. She pointed these areas out and reminded the riders to take their time.

"Caitlyn," the willowy woman called. "Is all of this your property?"

"Yes, as far as you can see from this point, but once we get a bit higher, you'll be able to view all the way to town."

"When I was a girl, I always wanted to live on a ranch."

"It's a good life—I have to admit." Caitlyn ran her fingers across Whiskey's black mane and wondered, not for the first time, if she had made a mistake moving away from the ranch. But she couldn't live under Dylan's thumb the rest of her life. She had to find her own way, even if she didn't know what way that was. Renegade led the pack, staying in front of the horses on their ascent up the trail. They'd ridden about five miles when the path meandered through a small meadow. Caitlyn stopped at the edge of the trees and dismounted.

"Let's stop here for a break. Everyone dismount, but keep hold of your reins. Now is a good time to get a drink, and if you like, you can get some terrific photos of the valley from here."

The three ladies climbed down from their horses and shook out their tired legs. "I sure am going to feel this tomorrow!" the older woman laughed as she stretched.

Herb ambled his way over to Renegade and crouched down. "Hey there, Renegade. You're doing a good job leading the trail ride, aren't you, boy?"

Renegade wagged his tail and, obviously having forgiven the man for his previous indiscretion, licked Herb's hand in return.

"I think you've made a new friend." Caitlyn approached.

"That looks like a nice camera." She pointed to the large device hanging around the man's neck. "I can hold on to your horse if you want to go to the edge of the cliff to see the view."

"Thanks." The man handed Caitlyn his reins and lifted his elaborate camera up to capture the expansive landscape.

A chilling scream sliced through the sunshine, darting ice slivers up Caitlyn's spine. She spun around to two women pointing at a shrub. Renegade dashed over to them and dipped low on his front paws like he was ready to pounce, barking furiously at whatever the women were gaping at.

"What is it? What's wrong?" Caitlyn passed the reins of the horses she held back to Herb and unclipped her sidearm on her way over to the women. They continued to point— frozen in fear. Caitlyn's gaze followed the direction of their trembling fingers. There it was. The cause of their panic. A diamondback rattler.

The brown, gold, and black snake coiled up tight, poised to strike—his quivering rattle standing on end. Caitlyn forced her voice to be low and calm. "It's okay, don't worry, he's too far away to reach you. He's just warning you he's there. Slowly, back away." The women took two steps backward before turning and sprinting back to the group. *So much for slow.*

Keeping one eye on the snake, Caitlyn addressed the tourists. "I rarely let a rattler live. They're too dangerous for our animals—especially my dog. I don't want to upset anyone, but I'm going to shoot him. Hold on to your horses, stand back, and cover your ears." Caitlyn never knew how city-folk would respond to the fact that they shot rattlers around here. This group voiced no objections, however, so she leveled her Glock at the snake, still coiled and hissing. She fired one round. After hitting her target, she returned to the riders. "Sorry about that."

The tall woman shuddered and rubbed her arms. "Are there a lot of rattlesnakes up here?"

"They're a little more active right now, in the spring, after their winter hibernation. Just keep an eye out." Caitlyn made a mental note to get Renegade to a snake training event again this year. He'd done a good job of warning without trying to play with the snake this time, but still. It was better to be safe.

After everyone had time to stretch out their tight muscles, drink some water, and take all the photos they wanted, Caitlyn called out, "Everybody ready? Let's mount up and finish our trek to the top of the hill. I'd like to take you up into the BLM if there's time."

"What's the BLM?" the slight, quiet man in the group asked.

"Bureau of Land Management. It's government land. Lots of ranchers pay the federal government to allow them to graze their cows up there during the summer months. We, at Reed Ranch, are no exception. It's beautiful countryside, and there's a waterfall up there worth seeing." Caitlyn waited for the more athletic folks in the group to mount their horses before she assisted those who struggled. She hopped on Whiskey's back and made her way to the front of the line. "Let's ride on."

Renegade took his position in the lead once again. Occasionally he darted off into the woods to chase a squirrel or rabbit. He zigzagged in and out, his coloring reminding Caitlyn of a fox. If she didn't know better, she'd wonder if he had some fox genes in him. Red on top, black face, belly, and long black legs—he was beautiful. As they made their last turn on the trail before the final climb to the BLM gate, Renegade stopped right in the middle of the path. He held up one of his front paws and his ears pricked forward. Tilting his head, he raised his nose, sniffed, and then bolted off in a sprint. Caitlyn chuckled and shook her head. Renegade loved trail rides.

Several strides further along, Caitlyn heard Renegade barking exuberantly. She pulled Whiskey to a halt and listened. Her dog was off to the left, in the woods about twenty or thirty feet away. Caitlyn turned in her saddle. "Everyone, please stay here. I'm going to ride into the trees and see what Renegade is barking at. It's probably nothing, but it's important for his training that I attend to his alerts. He's learning to be a tracker, and so I need to pay attention to what he finds, every time. I've trained him to stay at the spot where he's indicating until I come. So please hang out here for just a few minutes. I'll be right back."

"What do you think he found?" Renegade's new friend asked.

"Could be anything." Caitlyn reined Whiskey off the trail toward Renegade's alert. "Maybe a fallen deer or a dead rabbit, probably something like that." Renegade's barking echoed through the trees and bounced between the mountain slopes.

The terrain was rough and rocky, but Whiskey had no problem traversing the forest to where Renegade sat beside a large patch of turned, dark earth. Caitlyn wasn't sure what she was looking at. She dismounted, looped her reins over a tree branch, and hiked over to Renegade. "What did you find, boy?" She knelt next to him.

That's when she saw it, and her body recoiled. Partially covered with dirt was a delicate hand. *Is that... a human hand?* A chill coursed through her as she gaped at four blue-gray fingers protruding from the dirt as though reaching out for help. Caitlyn sucked in a breath. Without thinking, she stretched down and touched the fingers. They were slender, manicured in sparkling pink, and cold.

"Good boy, Ren." Caitlyn shuddered and her mind

swirled. She knew what she would do if she were alone. She'd race to the ranch and get help. But as it was, she had a group of inexperienced riders with her, and traveling down the mountain was often harder than going up. She swallowed hard against her insistent gag reflex.

Renegade whined as he watched Caitlyn's every move. "It's okay, Ren." Caitlyn reached into her saddlebag, where she kept a specific toy she allowed him to play with only as a reward. She handed it to him and tugged with him on it a few times before she released him to chew it on his own. She pulled her phone out of its leather case on her belt and took several pictures of the area. The dirt looked freshly turned, and the skin on the fingers hadn't yet decayed. Caitlyn snapped photos in each direction, then remounted her horse, and whistled for Renegade to follow. He trotted along behind her, carrying his rubber chewy in his teeth.

They found the group waiting for them on the trail. Caitlyn hopped off her horse again, took the toy from Renegade, and stuffed it back in her saddlebag. She turned to the others. "Maybe he should be a hunting dog." Caitlyn's false laugh sounded flat in her own ears, but she wanted to distract the riders and not let them know what she'd found. It would be dangerous to upset everyone. "There's a deer carcass up there. I don't know what kind of animal took it down. Could've been a mountain lion— could've been a bear. Either way, it's probably best for us to turn back to the ranch at this point, and not bother a predator's kill."

The tall woman reached forward and patted her horse's shoulder. "When I dreamed of a ranch life, I always imagined it would be safe. I'm rethinking my fantasy already. What with a rattlesnake, and now maybe a mountain lion, or worse."

One of her friends turned her mare around on the trail. "I

agree. I think it's time to head back. I'm fine with this being the turnaround point for today."

Herb turned his horse too. "Yes, we've seen some beautiful views and have had a lovely ride. But I think it's time to go back."

Relieved that she had convinced them so easily, Caitlyn waited for the rest of them to turn their horses around. Often, trail riders wanted to stay out all day. "Okay, let's return to the ranch. Let me get to the front of the line." She guided Whiskey to the downhill side of the group. "As we head down the trail, help your horse keep his balance by leaning back in the saddle a little. Just relax and let your body follow the horse's movement." Caitlyn was pleased that she could maintain a steady voice, even though her heart galloped through her ribs and her ears rang. She couldn't help wonder whose hand she saw and how the person came to be buried on the top of their ridge.

Caitlyn chewed at the corner of her lower lip and considered everything she had seen. They ambled down the trail at a decent pace, but Caitlyn had to resist the urge to push Whiskey into an all-out race toward the ranch. She was desperate to tell Dylan. To call the sheriff. To do something. But she held Whiskey at a slow gait so as not to alarm the other riders.

About two hours later, Caitlyn finally led the group through the barnyard and into the arena. Dylan stalked out of the barn. His brows knitted together as he gave Caitlyn a hard stare. "That was a quick ride. What are you doing back so soon? I didn't expect you before lunchtime."

Caitlyn communicated to him silently that something was wrong. She peered at him with wide eyes and wrinkled her forehead, but he seemed too irritated to notice her facial expression, so she gave him the excuse she'd told the tourists. "We ran into a rattlesnake, and then a recent deer kill. I didn't want to come across whatever predator had killed the animal, so we came back."

Dylan tilted his head and narrowed his eyes at her in question. "Is that so?"

"Help me dismount the riders so they can go on up to the ranch house. If Mom's not ready to serve lunch yet, I'm sure she'll be happy to get everyone a cool drink." Caitlyn stared meaningfully at her brother, hoping he would cooperate.

"How did y'all enjoy the ride?" Dylan deftly switched his gears over to charming—back to the brother she knew and loved. Cold relief flushed across her brow. Caitlyn worked side-by-side with Dylan, helping the riders dismount and find their way to the ranch house. Their mother met their guests halfway, and Caitlyn passed the group off to her before racing to the barn.

"Dylan? Dylan!" *Where is he?* Caitlyn ran into the red building.

Her brother stepped out of a stall, sliding the door closed behind him, and turned toward her. "What the hell, Caitlyn? Those tourists paid for half a day's ride. It's expensive. They should get their money's worth."

"I know, but—"

"But what, Cate? We have a reputation to keep." Anger glinted in his eyes as he stared at her.

"Dylan, listen to me. Renegade found a body. A dead, buried body! I didn't want any of those people to know. I was afraid they'd become too upset to ride back." Caitlyn grabbed Dylan's arm. "We need to call the sheriff. Now!"

"What? What are you talking about?" Dylan pulled away.

"I'm serious, Dylan. There's a fresh grave on top of the mountain, near the BLM gate."

"How do you know there's a body buried there?"

"Because it's a shallow grave. Ren was running through the woods and found..." She swallowed at the memory. "He found a hand. The fingers were poking out of the dirt." For the first time since she'd seen the hand, Caitlyn felt tears prick her eyes, and she ground her teeth against them. "I touched the fingers—you know—to be sure. They were cold. Dylan, we have to call the sheriff!"

Dylan narrowed his eyes like he didn't quite believe her, but he pulled his phone from his belt. "I'll call, then let's get these horses put away. Leave Whiskey tacked up, and I'll get Sampson. When the sheriff gets here, he can drive the ATV."

Caitlyn nodded and ran out to the arena to help put up the remaining horses. It took the sheriff over thirty minutes to get there from town. Finally, they heard his tires rolling across the gravel. The hood of his Jeep crested the last hill before the SUV descended into the barnyard. Sheriff Bruce Tackett and Deputy Colt Branson climbed out of the Jeep, simultaneously placing their dove colored felt cowboy hats on their heads as they stood. Caitlyn hadn't seen Colt in a while. Was it possible he was getting even better looking with time?

The sheriff adjusted his belt. "Morning, Dylan, Caitlyn. What's all this you called me about?" He peered at Caitlyn. "Dylan tells me your dog found a body?"

"Yes!" Caitlyn stepped toward him and thrust her hands out in urgency. "I was on a trail ride, and my dog smelled something. He took off and then sat down and barked. I went to find what he was trying to show me, and there was a grave."

"A grave?" The sheriff removed his sunglasses and stared hard at Caitlyn. Colt stood behind the Sheriff to his right and crossed his arms. Caitlyn couldn't read his eyes behind his mirrored aviators.

"Yes, well, I didn't know that's what it was at first. But then I saw a hand. Fingers poking right up out of the dirt."

Colt moved around the sheriff and addressed Caitlyn.

"Are you sure that's what you saw, Catie? Maybe it was an animal?"

Caitlyn glared at him. "I know what I saw, Colt." She pulled out her phone to show him one of the pictures she took. "That's not an animal. It's a woman's hand." She pressed her fists into her hips. "Do you think it could be Wendy Gessler's body?"

The sheriff mirrored her stance, resting his right hand on the butt of his gun. "Don't get all excited, now. We won't know what it is until we go have a look. As far as we know, Ms. Gessler is alive and well."

"Caitlyn and I will go on horseback, you two can take the ATVs." Dylan pointed toward the all-terrain vehicles parked next to the barn.

Caitlyn swung up onto her horse. "We'll meet at the trail-head, and Ren can lead the way."

Sheriff Tackett nodded, and he and his deputy made their way to the ATVs. Caitlyn glanced around for her dog, not sure where he'd run off to this time. It surprised her to see that he was already waiting for her by the arena gate. *He knows something's wrong.* "Let's go, Ren. *Stopa!*" Caitlyn used one of the Czech commands Logan had taught her, asking Renegade to track.

Renegade took off toward the trail. Caitlyn and Dylan loped their horses to follow him. Before long, the sheriff and his deputy caught up to them on their ATVs. They all stopped at the base of the mountain.

"It's a switchback trail and can be rocky in spots, but I think you should be fine on the ATVs." Caitlyn pointed the direction they would go. "I'll lead the way. It's almost at the top of the ridge. Let's go." Caitlyn turned Whiskey onto the path and urged him into a trot. In places, he bounded over tree roots and rocks, his powerful haunches rocketing Caitlyn up the hill. Renegade sped to the lead. When they got near the summit, he darted into the woods with Caitlyn on his heels. Her brother, the sheriff, and Colt joined her there.

Caitlyn led them to the shallow grave—to the fingers protruding from the ground. "Here, Sheriff, here's the hand."

Sheriff Tackett climbed down from his ATV and, followed by Colt, they made their way to the edge of the grave. "This appears to be freshly dug dirt." He knelt down and took a pen from his pocket. He slid it under the exposed digits and lifted them slightly. "Curious." He glanced up at Dylan. "How'd a body get way up here, do you suppose?"

"You're asking me?" Dylan crossed his arms.

"It is *your* property. I'm just asking if you know anything about this?" Sheriff Tackett unsnapped a leather pouch attached to his belt and pulled a rubber glove and a zipper-close baggie out. After slipping the glove onto his right hand, he lightly pinched the flesh of the hand. He stirred his fingers around in the loose dirt, finding something he dropped into the bag. Pushing himself to his feet, he scowled at Caitlyn's brother and held the bag up to the sun. Inside the plastic was an empty brass bullet casing.

Renegade curled his body around Caitlyn's leg, and she felt more than heard his low guttural rumble.

6

"**E**asy, Ren." Caitlyn reached down and stroked the top of her dog's head to calm him. The tension in the air was palpable. It wasn't surprising that it agitated him.

"What exactly are you asking, Sheriff?" Dylan crossed his arms over his chest. He glared at the lawman. "You know, just because this is my property, doesn't mean I had anything to do with this."

"It looks suspicious—all's I'm saying." The sheriff stuffed the evidence into the leather pouch and snapped it closed. He removed his sunglasses, pulled a corner of his shirt out from his pants, and cleaned them before re-tucking his shirttail into his tight waistband. "When did you say the last time you saw Wendy Gessler was?"

Dylan slid his hands down and propped them on his hips. "Look, Sheriff, just because there's a tree planted on my property, doesn't mean I planted it there." Dylan continued to glare at the big man, and Renegade's growl rolled, his hackles bristling.

"What makes you suspect Dylan, Sheriff?" Caitlyn's belly

tightened. She couldn't make sense out of what was happening. She glanced at Colt, who shrugged. "Why aren't you suspicious of me? I'm the one who found the body."

The sheriff shifted his steely gaze to her. "*Should* I suspect you?" He ran his fingers across his jaw. "I'm just trying to get an idea of what might have happened here. When was the last time you saw Wendy?"

Caitlyn shrugged. "I haven't seen Wendy for months." She watched Dylan from the corner of her eye, her gut telling her he'd seen Wendy much more recently than that. He'd acted funny when their mom asked them about her. He hadn't wanted to talk about the fact that he had dated Wendy before. But none of that made him a suspect for murder. She turned to stare at her brother full on, but Dylan wouldn't meet her eye.

"Let's go on down the hill, there's nothing more we can do here, besides contaminate the crime scene. We'll head back to the ranch. Then Dylan, I'd appreciate you coming to the Sheriff's Office with me." Tackett trudged to his ATV.

Colt's sandy brows knitted together, and he called out to his superior. "Are you arresting him, Sheriff?"

"No. Not yet, anyway. At this point, I just have a list of questions I want to ask." Sheriff Tackett swung his leg over the ATV seat. "As long as he comes willingly, that is." The lawman peered at Dylan. "If not, I can hold you at the jail for questioning for up to seventy-two hours."

"I'll come," Dylan murmured.

The sheriff nodded at the group and started his engine. "Deputy, you stay here and guard the crime scene until Doc Kennedy and a CSI from Gillette can get here."

"Yes, sir." Colt approached Caitlyn. "Are you okay?"

"I don't understand." Caitlyn pressed down on her rising panic. "The sheriff has no good reason to take Dylan into the jail. Why can't he just talk to him here at the ranch? I'm going to go to town with them."

"I don't need you to babysit me, Caitlyn." Dylan turned his horse toward the trail.

Colt ran his fingers down her arm and gave her elbow a gentle squeeze, causing goose bumps to rise on her skin. "Don't worry, you don't have to go with them. I've got this. As soon as I'm done here, I'll go back to the Sheriff's Office."

Her gaze moved from his hazel eyes to his mouth, and down to his square chin. When Colt was this close, it was hard to remember why she was angry with him. Her fingers still itched to comb through his sandy blond hair, even after all these years. "Well, you better do your job. I want Dylan home as soon as possible." Her tone was sharper than she intended. Probably due to the way he made her feel—all soppy and weak-kneed.

Colt stuffed his hands into his pants pockets and gave her a crooked grin. "It'll be okay, Catie. I promise to keep an eye on your brother when I get there and make sure he's treated fairly."

Caitlyn's cheeks prickled. "Sorry for snapping at you. I really do appreciate your help."

"No problem."

Renegade barked at the sheriff's retreating ATV. "Quiet, Ren." Caitlyn waited for Dylan to look at her, and when he finally did, she asked, "What do you make of all this?"

Dylan reached up for his saddle horn and stuck the toe of his boot in the stirrup. "I don't know, but it pisses me off. I guess I'll go answer the sheriff's questions. I have nothing to hide." He pulled himself up into the saddle and urged Sampson forward.

"Dylan," Caitlyn called out. He looked over his shoulder at her. "I don't know what's going on, but I'm here for you."

Dylan nodded at her and touched the brim of his hat before he rode off.

Caitlyn turned back, her eyes riveted on the gray, lifeless fingers resting in the dirt. *None of this makes any sense.* Caitlyn tugged at the corner of her lip with her teeth and ran through the facts that she knew—but she couldn't make anything fit together. At this point, they didn't know for certain who the dead body belonged to, or even if there was a full body. Maybe it was just a hand. She shuddered at the thought. They were all assuming it was Wendy, but it could be someone else. Too many unanswered questions.

Caitlyn reached for Whiskey's reins and climbed up into the saddle. "Let's go, Ren." She glanced back at Colt, who was stringing up yellow plastic tape that read, "Sheriff's Line. Do Not Cross." She waved at him before she turned toward the trail and urged her horse to catch up with Sampson.

By the time she rode into the barnyard, Sampson stood tied to the rail, still fully tacked, and the sheriff was helping Dylan into the backseat of his SUV. Her brother averted his gaze as he ducked into the dark interior of the car. Caitlyn jumped off Whiskey and ran to the sheriff's Jeep. Renegade followed her, letting loose several growling barks.

Tackett spun toward Caitlyn. "Get that dog under control, Ms. Reed. If he continues to be aggressive, there could be serious consequences."

"He's never bit anyone." Caitlyn choked on the sudden rage that inflamed her throat. "Taking Dylan in for questioning seems wrong, Sheriff. Does he need a lawyer?"

"That's his prerogative." The sheriff closed the door and made his way around to the driver's seat.

"You don't even know who that hand belongs to." Caitlyn glanced over her shoulder at Dylan and offered him what she hoped was an encouraging smile, before aiming her anger at Sheriff Tackett. "When is Doctor Kennedy going to be here?"

"That hand belongs to someone, Ms. Reed, Wendy or not. I'll call the doctor and the CSI office from my car. Don't let anyone go up there. If anything's disturbed, I'll hold you personally responsible."

"I think you'd do better to lay any blame for that at your Deputy's feet. You certainly won't be able to accuse Dylan because he'll be with you."

"No one is accusing him of anything. Yet." The Sheriff slid into his car and started his engine. Fuming, Caitlyn marched toward the house. The first thing she planned to do was to call an attorney. Tackett backed his Jeep into a two-point turn and drove out of the barnyard, kicking up rocks. Renegade's angry barking chased them down the drive.

Caitlyn whistled to him and when he came, she knelt down to stroke his head and soothe him. "What is it, Ren? What has you so upset?"

aitlyn rushed towards the ranch house with Renegade racing after her. "Dad! Dad! Mom!" Her mother flew out the back door and met her as she was running up the steps.

"What is it? Is somebody hurt?"

"Yes... I mean, no. Where's Dad?"

"What's going on, Caitlyn?"

"Follow me." Caitlyn rushed into the kitchen, the enticing aroma of baked apples and cinnamon barely registering before she ran down the hallway to her dad's study. She burst through the French doors and stood before her father's heavy wood desk. "Dad, the sheriff has taken Dylan!"

Her father stood abruptly. "Slow down, Catie-girl. Tell me what happened. I thought you were on a trail-ride?"

Her mom came around from behind Caitlyn, stood next to her husband, and they faced their daughter. "No, the trail riders are having lunch at the picnic table right now. I was just about to serve them dessert. Caitlyn. Tell us what's happened." She slid her hand down his forearm and linked her fingers through his.

Caitlyn took a deep breath and held it for a second before letting it out in a rush. "I was leading the trail ride today, and when we got to the top of the ridge, Ren found a shallow grave. There is a body buried up on the mountain, near the BLM gate."

"How do you know someone's buried there?" Her father gazed at her with a quizzical expression.

"Because, Ren sat down and barked until I went to see what he had found. I looked down where he indicated, and I saw fingers... sticking out of the dirt." Caitlyn blinked hard and swallowed. "I didn't want the trail-riders to know what he'd found, so as calmly as I could, I told everybody it was time to head back to the ranch. When we got back here, I sent the guests up to the house to find Mom, and I ran to tell Dylan what we found. He didn't believe me at first either, but he called the sheriff, anyway." Caitlyn took another deep breath and drew her bottom lip between her teeth. She met her father's gaze. "When Sheriff Tackett saw the hand, he took Dylan in for questioning. I didn't know what to do. The sheriff took him, Dad!"

A deep furrow formed between her dad's eyes. "Okay, calm down. I'll call the Sheriff's Office and see what I can find out." He released her mother's hand and gripped the receiver of the desk phone so hard his normally tanned knuckles went white. His jaw flexed as he jabbed at the numbered buttons.

"Are you okay?" Caitlyn's mom reached for her, worried blue eyes searching for reasons to fear. "I can't believe you found a body on our land."

Caitlyn hugged her. "I'm okay, Mom. Don't worry."

"We better move the tourists along. They're probably finished eating by now. Let's serve them their dessert so we can get them on the road."

"Can you handle that, Mom? Doctor Kennedy and a

Crime Scene Investigator are on their way. I want to be ready to lead them up to the gravesite." Caitlyn squeezed her mother's hand and without waiting for an answer, she and Renegade darted out of the office and through the front door. Caitlyn hoped to avoid the tourist group altogether on her way back to the barn.

A tan Nissan Cube drove up to the barn and parked. The driver, a short, compact woman who wore her straight, black hair cut into a no-fuss pixie, popped out of the door. She opened the back of her car and retrieved a camera and a portable toolbox. Then she reached in and pulled out a long yellow rectangle bag with a nylon strap that she slid over her shoulder.

Caitlyn and Renegade approached her. "Hi. Are you the crime scene investigator?"

The woman startled at her voice and blinked at her, but then smiled with a kind expression. "Yes. Are you Ms. Reed? I'm Officer Maeve Dunn." The woman held out her hand in greeting. "I'm supposed to meet the coroner here. Then, I was told, you could direct us to the crime scene." Her eyes darted furtively down at the dog.

"Yes. I've been waiting for you." Caitlyn shook Officer Dunn's hand. "This is Renegade. He's the one who found the grave. It's at the top of that ridge." She pointed toward the mountain. "You can't get up there in your car, though. Do you know how to drive an ATV?"

"Not a problem." Dunn glanced around, her gaze settling on the vehicle.

The women turned at the sound of an approaching vehicle. Dr. Kennedy rolled his thirty-year-old station wagon to a stop next to the Cube. The aging man pulled himself out of the car. "Hello, Caitlyn. How's the family?"

"Hi Doc. We're all fine. Thanks for coming out here. I wish it was under better circumstances."

"This is part of my job." He shifted the large black duffle bag he carried to his left hand and introduced himself to the CSI. "So, where is the body?"

"I was just explaining that you two will have to ride up the mountain on an ATV."

Officer Dunn nodded. "I'll drive."

"Great. I'll lead the way." Caitlyn showed them their ride, and while they loaded it with their equipment, she prepared Whiskey for their third trip of the day up the mountain trail.

The investigator and the doctor made a comical pair; she, stout and efficient, driving in front and he, round bellied with spindly arms, hanging on to her solid frame as they bumped up the path. Renegade bounded ahead, leading the parade once again.

When they arrived, Caitlyn tied Whiskey's reins to an aspen tree, and pointed the way through the pines shrouding the grave. "It's right through here."

"Please, keep your dog away from the crime scene." Officer Dunn called from behind her.

"Of course." Caitlyn asked Renegade to stay and led them to the roped off crime scene. "Colt?"

"Over here." Colt nodded a greeting to the town doctor and shook hands with Dunn. "I'm Deputy Branson. I've been guarding the crime scene."

"Have you started a crime scene log?" The small woman peered up at Colt.

"Not yet." He slid a thin notebook out of his front shirt-pocket.

"List everyone who has been to the crime scene and the approximate times of arrival and departure." Dunn set her equipment down thirty feet from the grave and went to work. She marked the perimeter of the area with a wheel measurer, then took photos from every angle before she retrieved her more detailed measuring devices.

Standing out of the way, Caitlyn asked, "Do you mind if I watch you work? I took a class on crime scene investigation in college, and I find it fascinating."

"I appreciate your interest," Dunn shook her head. "But it would be best if you went back home. We'll be down when we're finished. We've got it from here."

Caitlyn's shoulders fell with disappointment. "Okay. I should let you know you don't have phone coverage up here, and… watch for rattlers." A tiny zip of satisfaction darted through her at the fear that flashed in Dunn's eyes, then just as quickly, her empathy kicked in. "Don't worry. They mostly stay around the rockier areas. Just keep an eye out."

Doctor Kennedy and the investigator slipped on gloves, booties, and hairnets before Dunn methodically circled the scene. She wound her way closer and closer to the grave, looking for anything she considered potential evidence. "Here. This looks like a partial boot print. Not more than an edge, but I'm going to photograph and cast it before we move further." Caitlyn untied her horse and swung up into the saddle. "Come on, Ren. Let's go home." *Home… Will I ever stop calling this ranch home?* Together, Caitlyn and Renegade made their way down the mountain and across the pastures to the barn.

8

———————

Colt watched Caitlyn go. It was incredible to see her —to have this unexpected opportunity to spend time with her, though he was sorry it was under these circumstances. Normally, she avoided him whenever he saw her in town. He'd have to make the most of these chances because getting her out of his heart and mind had proved impossible.

He leaned against the trunk of a giant pine as the CSI proceeded with her work. She set up a tripod directly over the boot print and took photos at a ninety-degree angle. After that, she sprayed the impression with a soil fixative, then filled it with a casting substance. "That could easily be one of our boots, Officer Dunn."

The woman glowered at him. "Yes. It would have been helpful if no one approached the crime scene. There are dog prints here too." She frowned and cast them as well before taking twenty or more photos of the grave up close.

When she gave him the all-clear, Doctor Kennedy carried his duffle to the loose dirt and knelt down. "I presume you'll want to sift the soil for evidence as we uncover the body, but before you begin, I would like to bag the exposed hand." He reached for the fingers, pressed the skin and moved each joint. "Pliable. Past rigor. I'll check the core body temperature, but my guess at this point is that death occurred between forty-eight and fifty-six hours ago."

"That would make the time of death sometime Friday night into Saturday morning," Colt said more to himself than the others.

Doc Kennedy slipped a white paper bag over the exposed hand and taped it closed around the wrist. "Protecting any evidence that might be under the fingernails." He told them as he sat back on his heels. "Ready to sift through the dirt?"

Dunn retrieved a small spade, and a framed piece of screen. Painstakingly, she shoveled two to three cups of soil at a time onto the sieve and then jiggled the dirt into a pile beside the grave. Gradually she uncovered a woman's body.

The doctor took a core body temperature and Dunn snapped many more photos. When the investigator finished documenting the scene, Doctor Kennedy asked, "Deputy, we'll need your help to remove the body. Do you have gloves?" Colt slid on a pair and approached the grave as the doctor bagged the second hand.

"Here, rub some of this under your nose. It will help cover the smell." The doctor handed Colt a small jar of Noxzema. "Then, I'll get her feet, and you grasp her shoulders. On the count of three, lift and move her to the side. We'll roll her over once she's on level ground."

Colt braced against a shudder as he applied the sharp scented cream. This wasn't the first dead body he'd seen. It wasn't even his first experience with a fatal gunshot wound to the head, but it was the first dead person he *knew*. Kennedy would call Wendy's family to come in for an official identification, but it was her.

"Got some blood spatter here." Dunn sounded excited.

"And a lot of seepage directly below where her head was."
She carefully dug the soil and placed the sample inside a
large paper bag. Dunn collected several soil samples before
she sprayed the area with Luminol. With a portable black
light, she scanned the site to see how far the blood spray
extended from the burial spot. A wash of blue-green droplets
glowed in the dirt, and Dunn photographed and measured
it all.

"On the count of three, we'll roll the body to your right."
Dr. Kennedy counted.

"Look at all that bruising." Colt swallowed hard. "Was she
beaten?"

"Possibly, but this purple mottling is actually livor mortis.
When the heart stops beating, the blood settles at the low
points of the body. It's fairly even, leading me to believe the
killer did not move the victim after death."

"I concur." Dunn sat on her knees at the edge of the grave.
"With the blood seepage and spatter patterns I've found, I
think the victim was shot right here and then buried. The
shallowness of the grave makes me wonder if covering her
with dirt was an afterthought."

"Have you found the bullet, Officer Dunn? The entrance
wound is at the back of the victim's skull, and there is a clear
exit wound out the front."

"Still sifting."

"The sheriff already has the casing in evidence," Colt said.

Dunn's expression soured. She shook her head and
mumbled something under her breath before scooping more
dirt into her grate.

The doctor removed a heavy black zippered bag from his
duffle and spread it on the ground next to Wendy's body.
"Let's bag the body and seal it up. I'll finish my examination
at the clinic." He nodded to Colt and counted to three.
Together they lifted Wendy into the bag. Doctor Kennedy

zipped it up and sealed it with a labeled zip-tie. "I guess we'll have to transport the body by ATV down to the ranch where my station wagon is."

"Found it!" Dunn held up a wrinkled ball of metal with a large pair of tweezers. "Plenty of organic tissue still on this, Doc. The lab won't have any trouble making the connection." She placed the spent bullet inside a small paper bag to preserve the DNA.

Colt and the doctor waited with Officer Dunn while she finished collecting samples. It was late afternoon before she was ready to go. They strapped the body on the back of Colt's ATV, and slowly they descended to the ranch.

She was there, by the barn. Several strands of long chestnut hair blew in the breeze, having escaped her braid. If he wasn't transporting the dead, he would have stopped and watched her move through her chores—tough like her brothers, yet graceful as a dancer. His next whiff of the remaining Noxzema brought him back to the reality of the day, and he drove his cargo to the back end of Doc Kennedy's ancient station wagon. Colt helped load the body into the car and saw the doctor on his way.

Before she left, Officer Dunn explained she would take all the evidence she collected down to the Crime Lab in Cheyenne. "Expect a preliminary report from them in the next few days. Any DNA testing will take longer—that can take up to two months."

Colt thanked her and helped her get her equipment into her oddly shaped car.

"How did it go?" Caitlyn's voice curled like sultry smoke up his spine.

He turned to face her, taking in the light spray of brown freckles on the bridge of her nose. "Looks like it's fairly cut and dried."

Caitlyn's deep mahogany eyes searched his. "Was it Wendy?"

Colt shifted his gaze to the distant ridge and nodded. "Yeah. Don't say anything until the official report comes out, though. We need to let Wendy's family know first." He swung his focus back to her. "Now, we have to find the killer."

Caitlyn covered her mouth with her fingers, and her eyes misted. "It's so awful."

Colt rubbed her shoulder in comfort, wanting to pull her into his arms. He resisted, certain that her response would not be encouraging. "Can I ask you a favor?"

She tilted her head in question.

He smiled self-consciously. "Would you mind giving me a ride into town? I came with the sheriff this morning, but he left with Dylan." Colt's belly rolled like a river of leaping salmon as he waited for her to answer. After all these years, this woman still made him feel like an awkward teenager— all nerves and paltry confidence.

"I've got to feed the calves and the horses, but you can borrow my truck." Caitlyn stepped off toward the barn, shouting over her shoulder, "Keys are in the ignition. Bring it back with my brother." She waved without turning around and with pleasure, he watched her hips sway as she strode off.

Colt climbed into Caitlyn's pickup and took the forest highway to Moose Creek. The cab of the truck smelled like her. He ran his fingers over the various strings of things she had hanging from her rearview mirror and smiled at the seemingly random collection. Once he got to town, he made his way down Main Street, past the café and other shops, before pulling up in front of the Sheriff's Office. He parked on the street and entered the small brick building.

The office contained two desks and a single jail cell with a cot in the back-left corner. Behind Colt's desk, was a narrow cabinet with an old coffeemaker on the counter. By the smell of things, it was currently distilling the morning's brew into tar. Dylan sat in a wooden chair stationed in front of Tackett, who perched on the edge of his desk.

The sheriff looked up when Colt came through the door. "CSI get there alright?"

"Yes, they just left. How are things going here?"

"Slow." Tackett sipped from a stained coffee mug.

Colt approached Tackett and lowered his voice so only he could hear. "It's not for me to question your tactics, sir. But don't you think it's unusual to bring someone in for questioning who in all likelihood knows as little as you do—maybe even less? He probably would have been more cooperative if you questioned him at home."

"There is a history between Reed and Wendy Gessler. I want to put him off his game—find out about their past and see if he had anything to do with Wendy's disappearance. It's a mighty big coincidence that the girl goes missing and three days later a body is found on his property. Don't you think?"

Colt's abdomen tightened, and he cocked his jaw. He didn't like the direction of the sheriff's thoughts. He'd known Dylan and the Reed family most of his life, and it was hard to get his mind around the idea that Dylan had anything to do with Wendy's death. For now, Colt would keep the victim's identity to himself. He'd let the coroner do the reporting.

Earlier, Colt had wanted to comfort Caitlyn, and it wasn't simply her reaction that gave him pause. The truth was, he wasn't sure how it was all going to turn out. The one thing he could do was make certain things went by the book between the sheriff and Caitlyn's brother until he could take Dylan home. Maybe later, Colt would have another chance to ease Caitlyn's mind about the murder. Having her truck gave him the perfect excuse to see her.

"Tell me again, why you think I'm a suspect?" Dylan asked from behind them. He'd been angry when the sheriff wanted to bring him into the office for questioning, but it sounded like he'd calmed down a bit. Colt was glad about that, because it meant it was less likely something would go terribly wrong.

"I'm not saying you're a suspect," the sheriff answered. "I just have a few more questions for you."

"Well, finish asking them. I've been here all afternoon." Dylan leaned back against the chair and glared at Tackett.

The sheriff had handcuffed Dylan to the armrest. In one way, Colt understood the sheriff's caution. Dylan had a reputation for his short temper, and Colt didn't want to have to wrestle the man into the jail cell if things went south. The last thing he wanted was to get in a physical altercation with Caitlyn's older brother. But on the other hand, restraining a person who came in willingly for questioning could look bad in court.

"Sir, again," Colt whispered. "I'd like to suggest we follow protocol as closely as possible. I think we should un-cuff him. You never know what a sharp attorney might make out of the way Dylan is being treated. Cuffing him isn't exactly kosher."

The Sheriff's eyebrows shot up, and he raised his voice. "If we find out that the body belongs to Wendy Gessler and that Dylan here had something to do with that, we'll be the heroes of the day."

Colt narrowed his eyes. "That's a big leap, sir."

Having heard that part of their conversation, Dylan muttered from behind them, "It's a blind leap. I had nothing to do with Wendy's disappearance, or the grave at the top of the ridge."

Colt shook his head. "Sorry about this, man," he murmured to Dylan.

"Not your fault." With his chin held high, Dylan met the sheriff's gaze with a glacial one of his own.

"Deputy Branson, set up the recording equipment on my desk," Sheriff Tackett ordered.

"Yes, sir." Colt didn't want to be part of this, but he didn't have a choice. Not if he wanted to keep his job. So, he went into the storage room and found the decrepit recorder. The old piece of 20th-century junk wouldn't do half the job a simple iPhone would do, but Colt didn't bother telling the Sheriff that. The man still carried a flip-phone with no photo capability.

Colt set the recorder on the sheriff's desk, and his boss slid into his chair, glowering at Dylan. "Let's go over the questions again so I can record your answers." Tackett pressed a stubby finger on the record button. "Today is Monday, May 17th. Present in this interview are myself, Sheriff Bruce Tackett, along with Deputy Colt Branson. We are interviewing Dylan Reed regarding a dead body found this day on his property. We suspect the decedent might be one Wendy Gessler, a local woman missing since Friday, May 14th. First, and foremost, for the sake of the recording, I would like to state that Mr. Reed is not under arrest and has willingly agreed to this query."

"I'm not sure I agree about being willing," Dylan stated.

"To clarify, I requested Mr. Reed come in for questioning, and I drove him to the Sheriff's Office in my vehicle. At no time was Mr. Reed coerced to attend this interview." He shifted his gaze to Colt. "Do you concur, Deputy Branson?"

Colt sighed. The Sheriff's words were technically true. "Yes, Mr. Reed has been very cooperative."

The Sheriff tilted his head slightly and narrowed his eyes at Colt before picking up a stack of papers and leveling them with a snap on his desk. He lay them down and spread his hands over them. "Let's begin. Mr. Reed, how long have you known Wendy Gessler?"

"Since grade school, I suppose. I didn't pay much attention to her, but I knew who she was."

"But you paid more attention when she got older? Didn't you date Wendy after you two were out of school?"

Dylan regarded the sheriff for a moment. "I think we dated two or three times."

"Who broke it off?"

"There was nothing to break off. Like I said, we went out a couple of times. That's it."

"Were there any hard feelings between the two of you after that?"

Dylan shifted in the chair. "No."

"And you never took her out again?"

A shrug accompanied his answer. "Not really."

Tackett leaned forward. "Not really? What does that mean?"

"We live in the same town, so I've seen her around."

It occurred to Colt that Dylan hadn't exactly answered the question, but the sheriff moved on.

"Where were you last Friday night between the hours of four p.m. and midnight?"

"I spent the early part of the evening at the Tipsy Cow. I'm sure you'll find plenty of people who saw me there."

"Did you see Wendy that night?"

"Yeah, she was there."

"And you spoke with her?"

"A little."

The sheriff nodded smugly. "And the rest of the evening?"

Dylan hesitated, but he stared Tackett in the eye. "Then, I went home."

"And you can prove that?"

"My folks left for Gillette that night after dinner. They

57

JODI BURNETT

went for the weekend, so no one was home with me. My
mom called me on the house phone though, so I suppose she
knows I was there."

Sheriff Tackett sat in his chair and rested his entwined
hands on his belly. "That leaves several hours unaccounted
for then, doesn't it?"

"I had no reason to think I was going to need an alibi
while I was sleeping." Dylan leaned forward to brace his arms
on his knee, causing the handcuffs to jangle. The back-and-
forth between the two men was like a ping pong game that
had turned into a chess match. Neither opponent moved nor
spoke. Each seemed to contemplate the other's next move.

The Sheriff reached up and scratched his chin. "I'm sure
you didn't mind, Mr. Reed, that we had you stay here until
the CSI and the coroner completed their investigation of the
crime scene on your property. We should know by this
evening if that buried hand belonged to Ms. Gessler. Thank
you for your cooperation." Sheriff Tackett clicked the
recorder off before Dylan could record any objections.

"Dylan, you're not under arrest." Colt shot a glance at
Tackett before he continued. "You're under no obligation to
stay here. You're free to go anytime." Dylan held up his cuffed
wrist, and Colt used his own key to unlock the mechanism.

Dylan stood and shook his hand. "Thanks Colt, I appreciate that, but I'm gonna need a ride."

Sheriff Tackett nodded slowly. "Yes, that's fine. We'll take
you home."

Reluctantly giving up his opportunity to see Caitlyn, Colt
offered, "I borrowed Caitlyn's truck to get here. You can
drive yourself home, if you want."

The sheriff lifted his jacket from the back of his chair. "I'd
like to escort Mr. Reed home myself. It'll give us another
chance to look around. See what other evidence we might
find. Deputy, you can follow us."

CAITLYN BROUGHT the horses in from the pasture and fed them in their stalls. With the tractor, she dropped a 4 x 4 bale of hay into the feeder in the weaning pen and checked their water trough. When she finally left the barn, she saw the sheriff's jeep parked in the circle drive in front of the house. "Ren, *kemne*. Let's go see what the sheriff has to say." With a tingle of anticipation, Caitlyn wondered if Colt had returned with her truck. The sensation irritated her. She didn't want to feel anything for him. She reminded herself that he wasn't trustworthy, and she had no time for that kind of guy. But a wily smile curled her lips. *Even if he is still damn fine to look at.*

Caitlyn and Renegade entered the house through the back door, and immediately Ren raced through the kitchen to the front room. Caitlyn was quick to follow, and when she caught up to him, he'd raised his hackles and was growling softly in rhythm with his breath. "Renegade, *lehne*." Her dog reluctantly eased into a lying position, but the low rumble vibrated on.

Her mom and dad came from down the hallway and entered the room where Dylan stood between Sheriff Tackett and Colt. Caitlyn knelt next to Renegade. "It's okay, boy. What's wrong?" She nailed the sheriff with the fiercest expression she could manage, sweeping its intensity across the men to include Colt. "Couldn't find any evidence to arrest my brother with, could you? So you had to bring him home?"

Rising to the bait, the sheriff bit back. "The day is still young,"

Dylan's hands curled into fists. "I didn't do anything. There is no evidence that I buried that body on top of the ridge!"

"Besides, Dylan would never be stupid enough to bury someone on his own land." Caitlyn defended her brother.

"Stay out of this, Caitlyn," Dylan grumbled.

Renegade barked, and his lip rolled back, displaying razor sharp canines. *Something's not right. Is it Dylan's anger that's setting Ren off?*

"You truly have no business having an attack dog you can't handle, Ms. Reed." Sheriff Tackett scowled at her. "If he shows aggression towards us once more, I'm going to call animal control."

Caitlyn shot to her feet, but her father stepped forward, effectively blocking the space between the men and his daughter. "I think it's time for you to go, Sheriff. Thank you for bringing Dylan home."

Caitlyn, carefully avoiding Colt's gaze, snapped from behind her father's shoulder, "Yeah, but next time you decide to take someone into custody, you should have probable cause!"

"Oh, I didn't arrest him... yet." The sheriff turned toward the door and knocked into Dylan's shoulder on his way past.

Colt clapped his hand on Dylan's same shoulder, holding him steady and effectively preventing a physical reaction. "Sorry for all of this." He nodded to Caitlyn's parents. "Have a good rest of your night, Mr. and Mrs. Reed." His eyes sought Caitlyn. "You too, Catie. Thanks for lending me your truck. I'll call you later... if I learn anything."

Her cheeks heated under his gaze. She told herself the flush was due to anger, and she shrugged. "Whatever." She felt her mother staring at her, and Caitlyn clenched her fists, forcing her nails to bite into her palms to keep herself from squirming.

Her mom walked him to the door. "Thank you, Colt. We'd be grateful if you kept us informed."

9

Caitlyn's mother closed the solid front door behind the sheriff and Colt with a soft click and said, "I made a simple dinner. It's been a long day, and I thought we could eat together while we watch the news. This whole situation is upsetting, and I want to know what is going on."

Caitlyn glanced at Dylan, who was working his jaw as he stared out the window. She wondered what was running through his mind. "I'll help you mom." She followed her mother into the kitchen.

Caitlyn and her mom loaded trays with sandwiches, chips, and glasses of iced tea. On the way out, Caitlyn grabbed a plate filled with fresh-baked chocolate chip cookies, and together they carried the food into the great room. Her dad clicked on the TV and ran through the channels.

"Anyone hungry?" Caitlyn asked as she sat her tray and the cookies on the broad maple coffee table.

"Here it is." Her dad found the local news channel and set the remote down on the stone mantel. He took a plate, loaded it with sandwiches and chips, and carried it to his son.

"No thanks. I'm not hungry." Dylan stepped closer to the window, keeping his back to the family.

"You've got to eat, son. We'll get this all worked out." Their dad nudged Dylan's arm with the plate, and relenting, he accepted it.

The five o'clock news concluded the hour with the local high school sports report. Caitlyn figured news of the dead body would be the headline at six o'clock. She sat on the floor next to Renegade, who rested his chin on her leg and promptly dozed off.

"I wonder if the coroner has identified the body yet?" Her mother rested her plate in her lap.

Caitlyn took a bite of her ham and cheese, and mulled over what she knew of the case. She had promised Colt she wouldn't say anything, so she dodged her mom's question. "If it is Wendy's body, the official ID should come pretty quick. If it's not, then who knows."

"Sheriff Tackett said nothing about it while he was here," her mom remarked.

Eventually, Dylan took a chair at the dining table on the far side of the great room. "I doubt the sheriff will show any of his cards. He wants to believe the body is Wendy's, and that I killed her. It's gonna be up to me to prove otherwise. Which is bullshit."

"I agree, he's already biased." Caitlyn turned toward her brother. "But I can't figure out why. This is still America and you're supposed to be 'innocent until proven guilty in a court of law.'"

Dylan's mouth settled into a flat line, and he scoffed.

The musical theme from the newscast played, and the smiling face of Samantha Butler, the nightly news anchor, once again filled the screen. Using her serious broadcasting voice, she announced, "At the top of the news tonight, is the ongoing saga of the disappearance of Wendy Gessler, a local schoolteacher. A sad report in breaking news today; a body was found buried in a shallow grave at the top of a ridge on the Reed Ranch west of Moose Creek. We've just received word from the Sheriff's Office that a member of Wendy Gessler's family has confirmed that the decedent is indeed their daughter. Twenty-eight-year-old Gessler worked at the local middle school teaching history. Gessler had not been seen since this past Friday night. The dead woman's family has lived in the Devil's Tower area for generations. News of her death will come as a terrible shock for the entire community."

Caitlyn's mother gasped and covered her mouth with her hand. "That poor girl." Her dad wrapped one of the many Navaho blankets decorating the room around her mom's shoulders.

Caitlyn studied Dylan to gauge his reaction. His face remained as hard as granite, unchanging. But there was something in his eyes. She shuddered, remembering the cold, gray-blue fingers she'd found on the ridge. It seemed worse now, with the official announcement, that they belonged to Wendy.

The news cast flashed to an on-location camera and reporter who stood on the front lawn of the Gessler's' home. The shot was of Mr. Gessler with his arm around his wife, doing his best to maintain a stoic expression while Mrs. Gessler quietly wept into her hands. The reporter approached Jim Hague.

"This whole situation is awful," Jim said. "I can't believe Wendy is dead... that she was murdered."

The reporter inched his microphone closer to Jim's face. "Do you have any idea who might have done such a thing? Did Wendy have any enemies?"

Jim shook his head but then stilled, as though a thought suddenly occurred to him. He looked directly into the camera. "I don't know anything for sure, but the last time I saw Wendy, was last Friday night. She was at the Tipsy Cow drinking a beer with a man named Dylan Reed."

Dylan dropped his glass. It cracked and splashed tea on the table as he jumped to his feet. "That's a lie! That guy wasn't even there!"

Caitlyn spun around, waking Renegade from his nap. She gaped at her brother. "You were there? Last Friday? At the Tipsy Cow with Wendy?" Shock forced her to her feet. "You told Mom and me, you hadn't seen Wendy in weeks!"

All eyes in the room focused on Dylan. "I'd forgotten. We only talked for a few minutes before I left. We were *not* having a beer together."

"And people saw you with her?" Even to Caitlyn's own ears, her tone sounded accusing. She swallowed and tried again. "I think you better tell us exactly what happened last Friday night."

Dylan's eyes shot darts at her. "You can't possibly think I killed Wendy Gessler," he growled.

"Of course we don't." Their mother moved to Caitlyn's side and slipped her hand around her arm, pulling gently. "Do we, Caitlyn? That's not what you're saying, is it?"

Caitlyn couldn't look at her mother. She kept her gaze fixed on Dylan, watching his expression and the direction his eyes traveled. "What I'm saying is, we need to know exactly what happened last Friday night. Then together..." Caitlyn drew away from her mother and approached Dylan. "Together—we'll figure this out. Whatever happened, you're not on your own."

Dylan regarded her, his dark eyes as hard as flint. Caitlyn stared back, trying to read him. *Could my big brother really be a murderer?* She couldn't quite get her mind around the idea.

Jim's sobs drew their attention back to the news. The reporter was in his face. "Were you and Wendy at the Tipsy Cow together, or was she there with Mr. Reed?"

Jim pulled out a green bandana and blew his nose. He dabbed at his red eyes. "It's all just so tragic," he cried.

The reporter tried again. "Did Wendy leave the bar with Reed?"

"I just wish I could hold her one more time. I was going to ask her to marry me—and now I can't."

The reporter turned to face the camera. "There is still no official comment from the Sheriff's Office. Sheriff Tackett told us he'd have more to say at a press conference tomorrow afternoon. Until then, this reporter, along with everyone at Channel 6 News, offers our condolences to the Gessler family. Back to you, Samantha."

The bobble-headed blonde filled the screen once again and went on with other news. Caitlyn's dad clicked off the TV.

She reached for her brother's shoulder. "Dylan, listen to me. We're going to find out what happened, and no matter what, I've got your six." She squeezed. "No matter what."

Dylan acknowledged her with a lightning bolt glare.

10

Caitlyn and Renegade ended up spending the night at the ranch. It had been a difficult and emotional day, and Dylan refused to talk about the discovery of Wendy's body or what the news reporter had implied. Caitlyn spent her time trying to calm her mother and discussing the facts with her dad. The following morning, she sat with Ren on the front porch, sipping a mug of hot coffee with her feet propped on the rail. Renegade lay on the planks next to her tilted-back chair while she watched the white-gold sun stretch its arms into the new morning.

Tires sounded on the gravel and brought her to her feet. She peered down the road at the sheriff's jeep rounding the corner on its way up to the ranch house. Colt drove the vehicle into the circle drive and parked in front of the porch. Sheriff Tackett climbed out before Colt turned off the engine.

"I'd say good morning, but unfortunately that's not the case. Is your brother at home?" The sheriff rounded the car and stood at the bottom of the steps.

Colt stepped out of the Jeep, his expression apologetic. "Morning, Catie." He walked up the steps and knelt to pet Renegade. The dog's tail slapped the plank floor and after Colt received a wet tongued greeting, he moved back down the stairs.

"What do you want with Dylan now? You already interviewed him yesterday." Caitlyn balanced her mug on the deck rail and crossed her arms.

Tackett rested a boot on the bottom step. He took off his sunglasses and looked up at Caitlyn. "We've learned a few things since then. I'm sure you heard on the news, the body you found was indeed Wendy Gessler."

"What does that have to do with Dylan?" Caitlyn stared him down.

The sheriff cocked his jaw to the side and rubbed his chin. "That's exactly what we'd like to find out. Now if you'd be so kind as to let your brother know we're here, I'd appreciate it."

The front door opened, and Dylan stepped out. "I have nothing more to tell you than I told you yesterday, Sheriff."

When Tackett mounted the steps, Dylan moved toward him. The air between them crackled, and Renegade leapt to his feet, barking.

"Quiet Renegade. *Sedni*," Caitlyn ordered. Renegade quieted, and bent his hind legs into a sitting position, though he never fully sat down, his every muscle tense and trembling.

The sheriff glared at the dog before he continued. "We're here to take you in, Reed." He took another step toward Caitlyn's brother and reached for his arm.

Renegade lunged forward, snarling at the men. Caitlyn grasped his collar. "Renegade! *Lehne*!"

The sheriff and Dylan both jumped away from the sharp

fangs gnashing at them. Tackett pointed at the dog. "You better take that animal inside before I have him removed from the premises. I've warned you. He is a menace. A danger to society. I ought to have him put down."

Fury draped around Caitlyn's shoulders like a thick, black cloak, and she narrowed her eyes. "No one invited you onto our porch, Sheriff." Caitlyn tugged Renegade toward the front door. "He's just protecting our property and the people who live here." Caitlyn rushed her dog inside and closed him in her dad's office. She ran back out to the front deck, wanting to bear witness to any conversation the men had. By the time she returned, the Sheriff had handcuffed Dylan and was reading him his Miranda rights.

"On what grounds are you arresting him?" Caitlyn yelled. She ran down the stairs after them. Colt stepped forward and held her back.

"New evidence has come to light, Catie." He lowered his voice. "I agree with you, it's probably not enough for an arrest, but the Sheriff insisted. I promise I'll keep an eye on Dylan. But you should probably call an attorney."

Caitlyn searched his eyes and then turned to the sheriff. "What new evidence do you have?"

Tackett scratched his ample belly before propping his hands on his utility belt. "A hiker found Wendy's car abandoned on the forest highway three miles from your ranch road, and Doctor Kennedy informed us that Wendy was pregnant when she was killed." His words sent an icy shiver through her and she wrapped her arms around herself, rubbing goose bumps from her skin.

Dylan spun away from the sheriff. "How is any of that evidence against me?"

"That's what we want to determine." Tackett pulled Dylan toward the back seat of the Jeep. "You were seen with Wendy the night she disappeared. The location of Wendy's car gives you proximity, the pregnancy could be your motive, and the means... well... you have plenty of guns around here." The sheriff opened the door and placed his hand on Dylan's head as he pushed him inside.

"That proves nothing. Lots of ranch roads branch off from the highway. And even if the baby was Dylan's, it's not evidence of anything!" Caitlyn's mind raced along with her pulse as she tried to make sense of the recent information.

"Well, if Dylan agrees to take a paternity test, the results will surely tell us something. If he is the father, that could implicate him."

"The only thing that would tell us, Sheriff, is that he's the father. It certainly wouldn't implicate him in murder. I'm calling an attorney. I'm also calling Logan!"

The Sheriff chuffed. "You think just because you studied a little about the law in college and your brother is in the FBI, you can protect a murderer?"

"He's not a murderer!" Caitlyn ran to Dylan's door and pressed her hands on the glass. "Dylan, you don't have to take any test, and don't say anything until your attorney gets there, do you hear me?"

Dylan yelled back, "Do not call Logan. I'm serious, Caitlyn. Don't drag him into this."

The Sheriff brushed past her on his way to the Jeep. Tapping his fingers on the roof, he waited for his deputy.

Caitlyn grabbed a hold of Colt's solid arm. "This is insane, and you know it. You have no real evidence against him."

Colt covered her hand with his. "We'll sort all of this out, Catie. But we need to find the truth. You understand that, don't you?" His hazel eyes scanned hers.

He was right, but Caitlyn would have felt better if Colt would've sided with her. *Does he think Dylan is guilty, too?* All the Sheriff's supposed evidence was circumstantial. It would never stand up in court. Regardless of what Colt said, she worried the sheriff wasn't after the truth. He simply wanted someone to blame, and Dylan was the easiest target. Caitlyn released her grip on Colt's arm, and without another word, turned and ran into the house. She needed to call Logan and see if he could recommend a sharp attorney to defend their brother.

11

———

When Caitlyn slammed the door, Colt felt as though she'd slapped him hard across the face. He was in an impossible situation. He wanted to reassure Caitlyn, but if Dylan did murder Wendy, they had to bring him in.

He approached the Jeep and pinned the sheriff with his gaze. "Do you really think you have enough to hold him? It all seems inconclusive to me. I doubt you have enough evidence to make this stick."

Tackett glowered at him. "Whose side are you on? Can't you see past Reed's pretty sister to the truth?"

"Right now, I'm concerned about legal statutes. I care about the law."

"I want to get to the bottom of this too, but Reed wouldn't have come with us if we didn't force him." The sheriff opened his door and glanced back through the plexiglass separating them from their detainee. Dylan glared out the window. Colt slid behind the wheel of the sheriff's Jeep and turned back toward town.

As they all got out of the car in front of the Sheriff's Office Colt said, "Dylan, we just have a few questions we need you to answer, and if you want, we'll wait for your attorney. But if you would simply take the DNA test, it would make things easier on all of us." He took Dylan by the elbow and they followed the sheriff to the door. "The fact is, Catie's right, you do not have to agree to take that test."

"What are you saying, Deputy?" Tackett turned around, his face a mottled red. "Do I need to remove you from this case?"

"I'm just trying to do everything by the letter of the law, Sheriff. If you try to force Dylan to answer questions or take a test that he doesn't want, his attorney will have the court throw all the evidence out." Colt had been friends with Dylan and Logan practically all his life. He'd played football and baseball with the brothers when they were all in school. He wanted to believe Dylan was innocent, though he had to admit the evidence was pointing in his friend's direction.

Dylan narrowed his eyes at the sheriff. "There is no way in hell I'm taking that paternity test, and you can't force me to. Besides, why wouldn't you assume the baby belonged to that Hague guy? Last night on the news, he said he and Wendy were almost engaged. Did you make *him* take the test?"

"It's possible that Jim is the father, and we are gathering all the evidence we can." The sheriff jerked the door open and marched inside.

Colt looked Dylan in the eye. "Cooperation will go a lot further than fighting with the sheriff. Yesterday, you told us you only said a few words to Wendy at the bar. Had you been seeing her over the last couple of weeks?"

"I'm not answering any of your questions." Dylan glared at him.

He sighed and escorted Dylan into the Sheriff's Office. Colt undid one side of the handcuffs and directed Dylan to take a seat in front of the sheriff's desk before he clipped the open cuff to the chair. "We'll wait here for your attorney to show up." He brought Dylan a cup of coffee. "Listen man, I'm just saying, if there's no way that you're the father of Wendy's baby, why not take the test and prove it?"

"Because, I don't have to prove I'm innocent. You have to prove I'm guilty."

Colt considered his lifelong friend. "I hope to God we can't prove that."

THE SOUND of the slammed door echoed through the house. The force of Caitlyn's action chased away her sense of helplessness. Her parents rushed out of the kitchen. "What's wrong? Where's your brother?" her father asked.

Caitlyn answered as she headed toward the office to let Renegade out. "The sheriff and his deputy were just here. They arrested Dylan and took him back to town—to jail this time." She opened the door and Renegade waited politely for her to ask him to come out. "*Kemne*, Ren. You're a good boy. One of these days, I'm gonna let you bite that stupid sheriff." She turned back to her parents. "I'm heading home, and on my way I'll call Logan. I'm sure he can recommend a decent attorney. Besides, we should let him know what's going on."

"Will you call us as soon as you know something?" Her mother's eyes filled with worry, and she wrung her hands in a dish towel. With an equally concerned face, her dad slid his arm around her mom's shoulders.

"Of course." Caitlyn gave each of them a hug and a kiss before she and Renegade left through the kitchen door.

In the truck, Caitlyn slid her Glock out of the leather thigh holster she'd worn on the trail yesterday, and opened the firearm safe in the console. She cocked her gun, seating a round in the chamber and then re-filled the magazine before locking it inside the safe and driving away.

Once she was on the forest highway, Caitlyn switched on the radio. She absently tapped her thumb to the rhythm of the music before the morning news break interrupted her. The DJ's words barked out of the speakers. "We now have more information in the Wendy Gessler case." She turned up the volume. "As previously reported, authorities found Gessler's body buried in the mountains on Reed Ranch. Today, we've learned the coroner has confirmed that Gessler was pregnant at the time of her death. In a subsequent interview, Gessler's boyfriend, Jim Hague, stated that he suspects Mr. Dylan Reed of murdering Wendy. This morning, Hague implied Reed might be the father of Wendy's unborn baby. He stated Reed was the last person seen with Wendy at a local bar. Other witnesses have confirmed Hague's claim that the two looked upset during an intense conversation at the Tipsy Cow. Authorities are still looking for anyone who may have seen Reed and Gessler leave the bar last Friday night, either together or separately."

Caitlyn smacked her palm against the steering wheel. Hot coals stoked into a raging fire in her chest and scorched the backside of her eyes. Renegade sat up and cocked his head at her.

"I'm okay, Ren." She patted the silky spot between his ears. "But the shoddy reporting that's being allowed in this situation really pisses me off! Not to mention how unprofessional it is of the sheriff, allowing the boyfriend to try this case in the news." She reached for her cellphone and dialed Logan.

"Hey, what's up, Catie-did?"

Caitlyn's neck muscles relaxed a fraction at the sound of her second oldest brother's warm voice. "Hi, Logan. I have some crazy news for you, and I need your help." Caitlyn filled Logan in on the details.

"I can't believe this! I'll see if I can take some personal time and be on my way up there as soon as possible."

"There's nothing you can do right now. I'll let you know if we need you to come, but for the time being, I was wondering if you knew of a good defense attorney you would recommend? I'm deeply concerned that the sheriff is working under a confirmation bias. I get the sense he's trying to prove what he wants to be true and doesn't care about the actual truth at all. I don't think he's investigating anyone else."

"It wouldn't be the first time a law enforcement officer interpreted case evidence in a manner that confirms their own beliefs or theories. I'll ask around about a lawyer. Are you sure you don't need me to come up? I think I should."

"Right now, I'm just worried about Dylan's rights. I think the presence of an attorney will force the sheriff to run this investigation by the books. I don't believe he has enough evidence to hold Dylan. I'll let you know if we need you."

Logan was silent for a minute before he quietly asked, "Did he do it, Catie?"

It was Caitlyn's turn to pause. She sighed. "I don't know." This was a question she didn't want to face. "Dylan has been angry and defensive lately. He hardly talks to me. I'm doing my best to find out all the information I can. Colt promised to keep me up-to-date on any new developments. I'm going to figure this out. But either way, we stand by Dylan, right?"

"Goes without saying." He cleared his throat. "I'm glad to hear Colt is on the case. He's a good man and he'll be fair.

I'll call you with an attorney's name and number as soon as I get one."

Caitlyn promised again to keep Logan posted and signed off. She put her arm around Renegade and leaned into his strong shoulder. "We're going to do our own investigation on this case, Ren. Together, we'll find the truth, no matter what the consequences bring."

12

C aitlyn woke the next day invigorated, bubbling with more drive and energy than she had felt in years. It was as though it was a Monday morning, the first day of the month, the first day of a new year, in a brand-new century. She was eager to go—her purpose finally unveiled to her. She was going to do her own analysis and discover who murdered Wendy Gessler. Sheriff Tackett was supposedly investigating, but she didn't trust him for one second. All he wanted was a conviction and a feather in his cap. He didn't care if the man who went to prison for murder actually killed Wendy or not. And in this case, it was her brother whose life was on the line.

"Come on, Ren. It's time for a fresh start. We need to work on our training if we are going to be any good as a K9 team."

Renegade peered up at her out of the top of his eye sockets without lifting his chin from his bed. His expression seemed to say, *Don't drag me into your crazy ideas.* Caitlyn laughed as she dressed in her workout gear. "Eggs for breakfast, Ren. Breakfast of champions. You in?" Ren scampered after her into the kitchen where she prepared their meal; eggs on toast for her, eggs on kibble for him.

Outside, Caitlyn tightened her shoelaces. She estimated the run to the road and back was a full three miles, and she was raring to go. After some leg stretches and a few warm-ups, she struck out on the dirt road, Ren bounding beside her. She made it about halfway to the paved street before she had to stop. Caitlyn bent over, propping herself on her knees, and gasped for air. "Boy, Ren, am I ever out of shape. This is going to take longer than I thought." She ruffled his head and laughed as he sprinted ahead of her. For his part, Ren was in great condition. Caitlyn, on the other hand, finally accomplished the distance with a walk-run-panting combo.

Next on the training schedule was practicing Renegade's sniffing drills. Caitlyn rammed her shoulder against the door to her detached garage to open it. Inside, she searched through stacks of boxes and other sundry items. *Where did I put those cans of scents Logan set me up with?* There hadn't been a car parked in the building since she'd moved there, if ever, and the musty air filled with dust motes. She opened storage containers and rummaged around on shelves before she remembered she had placed the tins in the bottom of the tool chest to keep them safe. "Hey Ren, is your nose rusty? You should've been able to find these before me," Caitlyn teased. Ren cocked his head at her and barked once, his tail sweeping a wedge shape in the dirt on the floor.

Caitlyn reached into the tool cabinet and pulled out several paint-type canisters containing folded cotton cloths that Logan had doused with various scents. Some of them smelled of explosive materials, some gunpowder and ammunition, and others of different types of drugs. Caitlyn and Renegade hadn't practiced with these scents in months, and she hoped they were still strong enough to use. Logan gave her the kit when he helped her start Renegade's training as a pup. "Well, buddy? No time like the present." She gathered the supplies and carried them out to the yard.

Each can held two pieces of cloth. One to define the scent for the dog and the other to hide. Caitlyn would work with one scent at a time for today, asking Renegade to seek. Eventually he would be able to tell the scents apart and locate the one she asked him for. Caitlyn put her dog inside her cabin so he couldn't see where she hid the tin. She opened the sulfur scented gunpowder container and hid it under some brush about fifty feet from the house. She dragged the second cloth along the ground to mark the trail, then she went back to the front door and let Ren outside. She held the scented cloth out for him to smell. He sniffed and looked up at her, anticipating her command. *"Such, Ren. Such!"*

Her dog bolted forward and dropped his long nose to the ground. He zigzagged a few times before tossing his nose into the air and sniffing again. In less than a minute, Renegade found the hidden can.

"Good boy, Ren!" Caitlyn gave him the reward toy he loved to play with. She allowed him a few minutes of playtime before she returned him to the house so she could hide a different scent.

Renegade, once again, proved he didn't need as much practice as Caitlyn did. He hadn't lost his capability of searching at all. "Okay, smart guy. Forget practicing with one odor at a time. Next, I'm hiding all the cans at once."

She placed the containers in different locations around the property. Some she hid under pine needles, others in shrubs. She removed the ozone-like scent of cocaine from its tin and without dragging it on the ground, brought it back for Renegade to smell. The dog wiggled and drooled, watching every move of Caitlyn's hand, waiting for her to send him.

First, he discovered three cans that were not the correct

aroma, but he merely sniffed them and moved on. He knew what he was looking for. Then he ran to the farthest point where Caitlyn had hidden the cocaine-scented cloth. When he found it, he sat down and barked until she came.

"You are so smart, Renegade. Good boy. You've earned a break, and a treat." Caitlyn fed him a piece of hot dog and then handed him his favorite toy. Together, they went inside and Caitlyn prepared a salad for lunch while Renegade gnawed on his Kong. After lunch, Caitlyn took Renegade out to work on their agility and strength. She had no doubt that her amazing dog would do exceedingly well, though at this point, she questioned her own athletic capabilities.

The duo hiked out behind the house where Caitlyn had set up an obstacle course. Spring grasses and weeds had grown tall, but the course was there waiting to be used. She shrugged—perhaps running through the un-cut vegetation would be more realistic. At the front of the course were multi-level balance beams for both of them. Ren, behaving as if this were playtime, hopped up to the tallest beam and scampered along. He lost his balance once, but immediately circled back to the beginning and started again. Having learned, he slowed down and without a misstep, made it through. He sprinted to the next section with Caitlyn right beside him.

Next were a set of cross beam logs, four feet off the ground. They looked like a row of hitching posts. Renegade leapt over the first one, clearing it with ease by a good foot. Caitlyn braced her hands on the same bar and attempted to swing her legs in tandem to the side, up and over, the way Logan had taught her. Not a chance. She fell into the beam and scraped her knee. Shaking off the sting, she chuckled at her first effort, then kicked one leg over and pulled herself up the rest of the way before jumping down on the other side. For now, just getting over the obstacle would have to do. In a couple of weeks, she'd be clearing the obstacles like Logan could. Three more elevated logs to overcome. Renegade waited for her at the end of that section, ready to move on to the next.

When Caitlyn caught up to him, she laced her hands behind her head and paced, gulping air. "Give me a sec here, Ren, will you?" He barked and wagged his tail. The next-to-last goal was a six-foot wall. Six feet was nothing for Renegade. With a two-stride lead-up, he launched himself to the top of the fence, landed on his front paws and propelled himself over.

Caitlyn was happy no one was there to see the spectacle she made of herself trying to hoist her body over that same wall. Placing her hands on the top beam, she leapt up and caught her elbow over the edge. From that position, she pulled as hard as she could, swinging and kicking her legs until she got one heel over. Once there, it was easier to pull herself the rest of the way with the strength of her leg. But when she jumped down on the other side, she landed awkwardly, rolling her ankle. Bolts of stabbing electricity shot through the joint. "Schhhhheisse!" She cussed in German and tentatively walked it out until the pain eased.

All the while, Renegade waited for her at the bottom of the climbing rope that hung from a tree. Caitlyn laughed at him. "I'm not climbing that thing carrying you today, Ren. No way. I'll be lucky if I can get my own lazy ass up that rope." Caitlyn patted Renegade's head, and jumped as high as she could up the rope, gripping it in her hands. She wrapped the dangling rope around her leg, and she made it about three-feet further up the rope before she had to rest. She had nothing left. Sliding back down to the ground, she sat in the dirt next to her dog. "Well, it's just the first day. You're going to have to be patient with me, Ren. I'll get there. I promise."

Caitlyn took a long hot shower and spent the rest of her

afternoon creating a Murder Wall in her living room to assist her investigation. She hadn't hung any pictures since she'd moved in, so the location made perfect sense. She found a topographical map of north-eastern Wyoming in her truck, but after searching her kitchen drawers she couldn't find any tacks to stick it to the wall. She also lacked red string which she wanted to use for attaching related clues to each other, making it obvious at a glance which of them were connected, and how. And her printer needed new ink so she could print out the photos she'd taken of the gravesite. Catie made a list of the items she needed, then loaded Ren up into her truck and headed into Moose Creek.

Caitlyn's property was on the opposite side of town from her family's ranch, and it was about a twenty-minute drive before she saw the first roof-tops of the town's buildings. After cresting a small hill, she drove down onto Main Street. It was after lunchtime, so there weren't many people out on the sidewalks. She passed the gas station, the bookstore, and the café before she rolled past the Sheriff's Office on the far end of town. *I wonder how Dylan's fairing inside that little jail cell? Are they questioning him, or is he napping on that flimsy cot?* The questions she didn't want to ask herself were: did Dylan kill Wendy Gessler, and if so, why? She let her mind travel over all the things she knew. Remembering her discovery of Wendy's body, she scrutinized Dylan's subsequent reactions. He was the one who called the sheriff. Would he have done that if he was guilty?

Lost in thought, Caitlyn almost drove past the Mercantile. She swerved hard and bounced over the curb into the parking lot. She clipped on Renegade's leash and grabbed her purse. It wouldn't take that long to get the things she needed.

13

Caitlyn and Renegade entered the Mercantile and waved to the owner before making their way to the hardware section in search of a box of tacks. Finding a pack, she also picked up a roll of masking tape. One could never have enough masking tape. The small craft area was in the back corner of the store, and Caitlyn and Ren headed there next to find some red string.

"Well, if it isn't Caitlyn Reed."

Caitlyn looked up from her list to see Eleanor Smooter standing next to a younger woman about her own age, whom Caitlyn didn't recognize. The older lady's hairstyle—reminiscent of Betty Rubble from the Flintstones—was from a distant decade last century, complete with a little blue bow. "Hi, Ms. Smooter. How are you?"

Eleanor raised her pencil-drawn eyebrows at Caitlyn. "I'm sure I'm having a better day than you, dear." Her voice took on a sickeningly sweet timbre that set Caitlyn's teeth on edge. "I was so sorry to hear about your brother, Dylan." She cupped the side of her mouth with her hand and leaning in, whispered loud enough for the clerk up front to hear, "I hear he's in jail—arrested for the murder of Wendy Gessler."

Red heat flashed behind Caitlyn's eyes, and she gritted her teeth before responding. "The sheriff only took Dylan in for questioning, Ms. Smooter. We found Wendy's body on our property, that's all. My brother didn't kill anybody." Caitlyn tugged on Renegade's lead. "Come on, Ren. Let's go."

"I didn't mean to upset you, Caitlyn, dear." Ms. Smooter slid her large floppy arm protectively around the woman beside her. "But I had dinner with the sheriff last night, and Bruce told me he was going to put Dylan in jail for murder." Her dark eyes brimmed with challenge.

Caitlyn studied the younger woman standing by Eleanor's side, trying once again to place her. She didn't remember having ever seen her before. On impulse, Caitlyn thrust her hand toward the woman. "Hi, I'm Caitlyn Reed. I don't believe we've met." The young woman lifted her chin and glowered down at Caitlyn before she lightly clasped Caitlyn's outstretched fingers.

"This is...my house guest, Maribel Martin. She's visiting from Nebraska." With her arm still around Maribel's shoulders, she pulled the woman close. Maribel's sweater fell open and Caitlyn couldn't help but notice her pregnancy.

"Welcome to Moose Creek, Maribel. Maybe I'll see you around." She gave a curt nod to Eleanor and strode away. *I'd forgotten Eleanor Smooter and Sheriff Tackett were an item. I need to come to town more often if I want to stay caught up with the local gossip.*

Caitlyn found the red string and the other items on her list, paid, and went back out to her truck.

"Caitlyn! Catie!" She snapped her head around to see who was calling her. Colt waved at her from up the block. He jogged toward her, and she raised her hand to wave in return. "Wait up."

Caitlyn opened her truck door and Renegade sprang inside. She placed her shopping bag on the floor and with her heart hammering, she turned to wait for Colt.

"I didn't know you were coming into town today." Colt draped his arm from the top of the door and leaned against it.

Caitlyn raised an eyebrow. "I didn't realize I was supposed to tell you when and where I'm going."

Colt's face bloomed into a bashful grin. "No, of course not. I'm just surprised to see you, that's all."

God, that smile will be the end of me. "How's Dylan?"

"He's as mad as a wet cat and still refusing to take a paternity test. Hague has agreed to take one, though."

Frustration strained her words. "I told all of you to wait until Dylan had a chance to talk with an attorney."

"I know, but Dylan told me there was no way he could be the father, so I figured what harm could it do?"

"That's not the point, Colt."

He perched his hands on his hips and gazed down at the ground. When he looked back up, Caitlyn saw concern written across his chiseled features. "I'm sorry about all this, Catie. Can I buy you a cup of coffee?"

Caitlyn needed Colt's help if she was going to run any kind of proper investigation. There was bound to be information she could only get from him. At least that's what she told herself when she answered. "Sure, okay. That would be nice. I need to see when I'm scheduled for my next shift at the café, anyway." She called Ren to hop out of the truck, and when he did, he rubbed up against Colt's knees, wagging his tail. Colt reached down and ruffled Ren's tall pointy ears. Together, the three of them walked up to the café.

They chose a booth in the back, away from the windows near the sidewalk, in a vain attempt to not broadcast their meeting. Of course, this was a small town so everyone and their horse would know Caitlyn had coffee with Colt by dinnertime. Renegade curled up underneath the table and resting his chin on top of Caitlyn's boot, he settled in for a snooze.

She blew across the shimmering surface of her coffee and regarded the sharp angle of Colt's square jawline. "Do you have any new information concerning the case?"

He wrapped his hands around his warm mug and stared into it, perhaps hoping answers would float up in the steam. Eventually, Colt lifted his gaze to Caitlyn. "I really shouldn't discuss the case with you."

Caitlyn leaned back against the booth. "I suppose I ought to tell you, I'm running my own investigation."

"What?"

"You heard me. I don't trust Sheriff Tackett to give Dylan a fair shake. All he cares about is pinning Wendy's murder on someone—anyone. Whether that person is actually guilty is of little consequence to him. Tackett just wants to look good for the voters." She leaned forward on her arms and gazed into Colt's bluish-green eyes. "But the person he wants to blame, is my brother. I have to help him. Don't you see?"

"Absolutely not, Catie." His gaze never wavered.

Caitlyn resumed her previous position, pressed back against the booth. "I don't recall asking your permission." They considered each other for a while before Caitlyn changed tack. "I saw Eleanor Smooter in the Mercantile this afternoon. I had forgotten she was dating the sheriff."

Colt responded with a one-shoulder shrug. "So?"

"So, she practically shouted to the entire store that Dylan was at the jail—spouting out how he was going to be arrested for murder. No doubt she got that little tidbit from Tackett." She speared him with a pointed look. "Apparently, it's okay for *him* to discuss the case with others." Caitlyn leaned forward and reached for Colt's wrist. She gave him a gentle squeeze. "Look, if I could trust the sheriff to be fair and do a thorough investigation, I wouldn't have to do it myself. But we both know I can't."

Colt dropped his gaze to Caitlyn's fingers. She watched the muscles in his jaw working as he thought over what she said. Eventually, he looked back up into her face, his eyes filled with a wary sort of yearning. "I think you're being a little hard on Sheriff Tackett. He's trying to do his job. But if you're determined to do this, I'll try to help you the best I can." He looked back at her hand on his arm. "As long as you understand, there will probably be things I won't be able to discuss." He covered her fingers with his.

Alarm bells rang between Caitlyn's ears. She pulled her hand away from him. "I'd like your help, but that doesn't mean anything has changed between us. I need to make that perfectly clear." Her heartbeat ricocheted between her ribs. She was torn between wanting his hand on hers and running from him along with the pain she knew he was capable of causing her.

The green in his eyes deepened, and an almost imperceptible sigh escaped Colt's chest. "Why can't you forgive me, Catie? What happened was a long time ago. We were just kids—*I* was a stupid kid."

"Maybe, but you really hurt me. Cheating is a deeply rooted character trait. One that comes from your core. You don't get second chances after that—not with me. Especially after we…" Caitlyn let her words trail off. She didn't have the emotional energy to debate this with him again. "Look, right now, all I want to focus on is finding Wendy Gessler's murderer."

"And if it turns out to be Dylan?"

"I need to know the truth. Either way."

"Okay, Catie. We'll do this your way. But I'm not giving up on resolving us."

"There is no us." Caitlyn wasn't about to dredge up all that pain again. Ever. No matter how often she thought about nestling into Colt's broad chest and finding comfort in the strength of his arms.

14

Before they left the café, Colt had convinced Caitlyn to let him bring dinner to her house later that night, winning her over by assuring her it would be a working meal. He picked up Chinese takeout from Wong's Kitchen and drove out to Caitlyn's new place, bumping along the dirt road to her cabin. Renegade barked a warning, but he soon recognized Colt's Jeep and wagged his tail in greeting. Colt pulled up next to Caitlyn's truck, and when he opened his door, Renegade was there dancing at his feet.

"Hey, buddy." He reached down and scratched the dog behind his ears. "I'm glad to see you, too." Colt made his way up the front steps, doing his best not to trip on his canine escort. He rapped three times on the solid wood door.

Muffled steps sounded inside before the door opened about six inches. Caitlyn held the door with one hand and peered out through the crack. "Hi."

Colt could practically touch the apprehension floating in the air around her. "Hi." He held up the bags of food. "I have Kung Pao Chicken. Are you hungry?"

Caitlyn gazed at him for a few heavy seconds, before she opened the door the rest of the way to let him in.

"Where should I put this?" Colt glanced around the room. There was a cozy fire blazing in a stone fireplace in a sitting area on the left. The open space merged into the kitchen on the right. On the far wall, behind a small dining table where a painting should go, he noticed that Caitlyn had pinned up evidence regarding the Gessler case. He swallowed a grin and instead set the bags of food on the counter bar that divided the kitchen from the living room.

"That smells good. I didn't realize how hungry I was until right now." Caitlyn followed him to the kitchen and moved past him to pull dishes out of the cupboard. "We can fill our plates and eat in front of the fire, if you want? What would you like to drink?"

"Beer for me, thanks." While Caitlyn reached for two bottles in the fridge, Colt busied himself filling their plates. Together they carried their meal to the coffee table in front of the warm fire. It was May, but the evenings were still cold enough for them to appreciate the extra heat. They ate in silence for several minutes, listening to the flames crack and pop before Colt broached the uncomfortable topic.

"Catie, I know you don't want to talk about this, but I'd really like to start with a clean slate. I can't tell you how sorry I am for being an idiot all those years ago. I know I hurt you, but that was the last thing I ever intended. I wasn't thinking. I was just a stupid seventeen-year-old full of hormones." Colt pleaded with her, watching for any sign of reprieve.

Caitlyn considered his words while she finished chewing her mouthful, staring at him for a moment before she answered. "That's not good enough, Colt. I trusted you. I believed you loved me. I shared *everything* with you. How could you tromp on that, and blame your actions on hormones? What? I just slipped your mind? You really hurt me—more than you know." She lowered her chin and her shoulders curled in protectively. She spoke toward the floor. "I loved you, Colt, and you broke my heart." She looked up at him from the corner of her eye. "And I never intend to let that happen again."

"Catie…" He reached for her hand.

Caitlyn stood abruptly and moved to the fireplace. She steadied herself by holding onto the raw-edge wooden mantel. "You're here tonight so that we can discuss the murder case. That's it. If you plan on bringing up personal history all night, you may as well leave now."

Colt held up his hands in surrender. "Okay, I get it. Where do you want to begin?" His chest ached like he'd been kicked—still, if this was all he could have, he'd rather be here with her talking about a murder than anywhere else.

Caitlyn studied him for a second before she picked up her plate and walked over to her wall of evidence. "This is what I have so far."

In the center of the wall, she had tacked up a piece of paper with the question, "Who Murdered Wendy?" She circled the words in red ink. Above that was a timeline marked with key dates, including the Friday when Wendy was last seen, through the following Monday when her body was found. Caitlyn had added the arrival of the CSI and coroner, the approximate time the sheriff received the Coroner's preliminary report, and the date and time of Dylan's arrest.

On the left side was a sheet of paper titled "Suspects" under which she'd written Dylan's name. On another sheet titled "Physical Evidence," she recorded the location of the body in the shallow grave, the casing Sheriff Tackett found, and the fact that Wendy had been pregnant. Under "Witnesses" on the right side of the wall, Caitlyn had jotted down that Jim Hague allegedly saw Dylan having an intense conversation with Wendy at the Tipsy Cow the night she disappeared. With red string, she had connected the events on the timeline with their coordinating items on the board below.

Caitlyn pointed to the map pinned on her wall. "This is a topographical map of Reed Ranch and the surrounding acreage. I've circled the location where I found Wendy's body and sketched the path from that location back to the ranch." She picked up a red pencil and pointed at the map. "Here, approximately thirty yards from the location where her body was buried, is a gate to the BLM that borders our property."

"Why do you have a gate from your property to the BLM? It's not big enough for cattle." Colt carried his plate over and joined her at the wall.

"We like to ride up into the BLM whenever we can. It's gorgeous countryside." She pointed to another location on a flatter section of the ranch land. "Down here is our double gate. It's wide enough to push our herds through for grazing them on the BLM in the summer. We only use the gate near where the body was found for hiking or trail-riding."

"It seems to me, that someone on the ranch would have noticed a stranger driving through your property up that trail to the location of the grave. Who else knows about the gate?"

Caitlyn nodded thoughtfully. "I'm not sure. But if no one was home at the time, someone could go up there and back completely unnoticed." She tapped her chopsticks against the fingers of her other hand. "Obviously, Dylan had the opportunity that night to go up there without being seen since my parents weren't home." A furrow formed between her brows. "I just can't imagine Dylan killing someone. And if he did, would he be stupid enough to bury the body on his own property?"

"It might have been a temporary gravesite since it wasn't

very deep." Colt scanned the other items on the wall. "What else do you have?"

"I have these photos of the gravesite. I took them with my phone. These three," Caitlyn pointed to the top row of photos, "I took when I first found the body." She indicated several more in the row below. "These I took when Dylan and I showed you and Sheriff Tackett what we found."

"We ought to have copies of these photos at the Sheriff's Department."

"TAKE YOUR OWN PHOTOS. You're supposed to be the professionals." Wondering, belatedly, if it was a good idea to share all she knew with him, Caitlyn moved off to the side and read from a sheet of paper tacked on the edge. "These are the few facts as I know them: One, Wendy had not been dead long when Ren discovered her grave. We know this because several people reported seeing her at the Tipsy Cow on Friday, and I found her body on Monday morning." Caitlyn chewed on the end of a chopstick. "Two, whoever buried her was in a huge hurry."

"Why do you say that?"

"Because the killer didn't take time to dig a deep grave or cover her carefully. Like you said, it may have been a tempo-rary solution. Frankly, I'm surprised we found her before a forest animal did." Caitlyn leaned against the table and Colt joined her there. His warmth was magnetizing, so she took a step away from him to the side. "And three, we know Wendy was pregnant, but at this point we don't know who the father is, or whether the pregnancy had anything to do with her murder. If not, what other motive might someone have had to murder Wendy Gessler? Which leads me to ask why Dylan was arrested? What possible motive could *he* have?" Caitlyn pinned Colt to his spot with her eyes as she waited for an answer.

"Don't you think it's suspicious that Dylan refuses to take a paternity test? If he was innocent—if there was no possibility of him being the father—why wouldn't he just take the test?"

"No, Colt, you're taking a shortcut in your thinking. It may seem obvious to you at first, but don't you see? You're missing crucial elements in your theory... You have tunnel vision because you're trying to make the evidence fit who you think is guilty, instead of allowing it to point you to the actual murderer. Besides, it isn't up to Dylan to prove he's innocent." She paced back and forth in front of her evidence board. "And, even if he is the father, that wouldn't automatically give him a motive to kill her."

"Wendy's parents asked Hague if he would take a paternity test, and he did. We should have the results of that test tomorrow. That should tell us something."

"Still, I can't see how her pregnancy would give anyone a motive to kill her. Jim announced on the news the other night that he had been planning to ask Wendy to marry him."

"What if Wendy was pregnant with Dylan's baby, and Dylan wanted her to have an abortion, but she refused? That could be a motive."

"No way. You know Dylan better than that, and so do I. He would never ask her to do something like that. Wendy being pregnant with his baby would not make him want to kill her."

"Then explain why Dylan has been so moody and angry for the past several months."

Caitlyn stared at Colt, thinking over the facts, and her heart burned at his words. "How far along was Wendy? Did the doctor say?" Caitlyn's gaze drifted back to the evidence board.

Colt chewed a bite of spicy chicken and took his time to swallow. "I could lose my job if I tell you what was in his report."

"You know you can trust me not to tell anyone, and besides, I'm sharing everything I know with you. I'm just wondering about the timing. You see, I know why Dylan has been a jackass for the past couple of months, and it has nothing to do with Wendy. Dylan is mad at me. He's been mad at me all along, and it isn't about Wendy or anyone else."

"Why is he so mad at you?" Colt set his plate down and crossed his arms over his chest.

"It's family stuff. It's no one else's business, and it has nothing to do with this case."

"Why don't you let me be the judge of that?"

"I've already judged it, and it isn't any of your business."

Colt sighed. "You want me to trust you, Caitlyn, but you refuse to trust me. That isn't fair."

"One doesn't have to do with the other, Colt."

"Trust is trust." His sandy brows crunched together, framing the flecks of icy blue-green irritation in his eyes.

"Fine! Dylan is mad at me for a decision I made that ended up putting the ranch in a financial mess." Caitlyn snatched up her beer bottle and took several swigs.

"What possible decision could you have made that would do that? And do you think Dylan is mad enough about that to hurt you?" Colt's worried eyes watched her carefully while he waited for her answer.

To create some space between them, Caitlyn moved to the living room and jabbed at the ebbing fire with a poker. She leveled out the smoldering logs, making room for a new one, and tossed in a chunk of pine that caught instantly. With a ragged breath, tears she'd been holding at bay, nurtured by raw guilt, scorched the back of her eyes and pressed until they overflowed, coursing down her cheeks. She rubbed her face on her sleeve.

"Last summer, I asked my dad to give me my third of the ranch inheritance in cash so that I could buy a place of my own." Her heart ached as she appealed to Colt for understanding. "You see, Dylan is the only one of us kids who wants to run the ranch. One-third of its worth will be mine, and the other third will be Logan's. But the thing is, I don't want to live there for the rest of my life. My only job prospect would be working as a ranch hand for my big brother. I'd never be able to afford my own place doing that."

"Anyway, my dad agreed. Unfortunately, he had to take an equity loan out against the ranch to get the cash. The loan raised the mortgage payment and made things really tight, and when Dylan didn't get the price he needed for the cattle he sent to the market last fall, what was financially tight became strangulating."

"What do you mean by strangulating?"

"Dylan is at risk of losing the ranch altogether, and it's all because of me. So you see, he has every reason to be angry with me. Hell, I'm angry at myself. But what can I do now? I already spent the money on this place." Caitlyn's throat tightened over her voice as she fought off more tears. Pausing, she swallowed hard. "What's done is done, but if it comes down to it, I'll sell this place and give the money to Dylan. There's no way I'll let him lose that ranch."

"Does Dylan know that?"

"No! He won't listen to me. He refuses to talk to me about it." Caitlyn slammed her bottle down on the dining table, causing the beer to foam out the top.

"Do you think you could be in danger? Is Dylan mad enough to hurt you?"

"Dylan would never hurt me." Caitlyn gazed into the fire.

She hoped she was right, but then again, she'd never seen such fury in her brother's eyes before.

COLT HAD KNOWN Dylan a long time. He was a man of few words and powerful emotions. The one thing the man loved more than anything else was that ranch. Colt wasn't convinced at all that Dylan wouldn't hurt Caitlyn. He wasn't convinced that Dylan was innocent of murder, either. An unexpected baby and the financial obligations that came with it could send a desperate man over the edge.

The one thing Colt knew at this point was that he was determined to keep Caitlyn safe. The only way he could see himself doing that, if they released Dylan, was by staying close to her, and his excuse to do so would be her investigation. "I have one thing I can tell you about that we learned from Doc Kennedy that has not been broadcast on the news."

Caitlyn turned and searched his face with her deep brown eyes. "What? What did you learn?" She moved toward him.

"The cause of Wendy's death." Caitlyn held her breath, waiting. "Wendy was shot in the back of the head, execution style. The investigative team believes the perp shot her on location, at the side of the grave. There was evidence of blood spatter in the surrounding soil."

Caitlyn stared at him. "The murderer took Wendy to the top of the ridge while she was alive?" She rolled her lower lip in between her teeth and bit down. Her eyes took on a distant glaze, and she resumed her pacing. "There was no sign of a struggle near the grave. Presumably, whoever took her up to the ridge was someone she knew and trusted. It could have been Dylan, but why? I don't see a surprise baby as something he would kill over. You know Dylan, he's the type who would offer to marry her."

"But what if she wanted money? Money he didn't have?"

Caitlyn seemed to consider that possibility, then continued. "Who else might have a motive? Jim seems the obvious choice."

"Yeah, except that Jim willingly went along with having a paternity test and he has answered all sorts of questions regarding Wendy. It's Dylan who refuses to cooperate." A heavy, cold lump formed in Colt's belly.

CAITLYN'S THROAT ACHED. Her shoulders drooped, and she lowered her chin to her chest. Her body shook with silent tears and Colt rushed to her. He pulled her into his arms, and she didn't resist. In fact, she returned his embrace, sliding her hands up the defined muscles of his back, seeking solace in his comforting warmth. When her tears were spent, she looked up into Colt's face. Compassion filled his kind eyes, and she gave him an embarrassed smile. He bent down, his gaze dropped to her mouth, and his lips followed.

A starved flame of desire leapt inside Caitlyn's body, overshadowed only by a deep yearning to be loved. Colt smelled of leather and fresh air. He cupped the back of her head in his hand, but when his lips met hers, Caitlyn's spine instinctively stiffened. She pushed away from him, taking deep breaths to help her maintain her resolve. "This can't happen, Colt. I think it's time for you to go." She pointed at the door.

"I'm sorry, Catie. I didn't mean for that to happen." His jaw stiffened, and he hung his head. After a breath, he returned his gaze to her. "Can we just forget it and finish talking about the case?"

"We've talked enough for tonight." She needed him to leave. Caitlyn fought hard against the temptation of his kiss when everything inside her demanded more. She didn't want him to realize how difficult it was for her to tell him to go.

Silently, Colt appraised her. Finally, he gave his head a shake, turned to the table to pick up his hat, and strode to the door. At the threshold, he turned back. "I'll call you tomorrow when I find out the results of Hague's paternity test."

Caitlyn nodded, but she couldn't speak. Her roiling emotions were a hot mess. Worry for Dylan, fear for the ranch, and the intense feelings she refused to acknowledge for Colt, but that warred against her heart, all jumbled together in a massive wad.

"Good night." Colt reached down and gave Renegade a farewell pat before he walked out.

Caitlyn closed the door behind him and on her way to study her evidence wall, she grabbed another beer. Packing her emotions neatly back inside, she pulled a dining room chair over, centered it before the wall, and sat. Renegade lay at her feet, and resting his chin on her foot, released a long-suffering whine.

"I know you love him, Ren, but that doesn't make him good for me. Let it go, bud."

Renegade sighed.

From her position on the chair, she studied at the facts she knew at this point, while she slowly sipped the malty brew out of her fresh bottle. In her heart, she couldn't imagine Dylan as a murderer. But it was possible that he was already feeling trapped by his responsibilities to a struggling ranch when Wendy told him she was carrying his baby. Maybe she did make financial demands he didn't think he could manage. Still, that didn't seem like enough reason to kill someone. Plus, if Dylan was going to shoot somebody, he would never shoot them in the back. He was a lot of things, but a coward wasn't one of them. She sucked in another thoughtful swallow of beer.

But if not Dylan, then who? When someone gets murdered, the most obvious suspect is a spouse. Wendy wasn't married, but she was about to become a mother. Whoever the father was should definitely be considered a suspect. That manner of thinking brought her back to Dylan... and Jim.

Jim appeared distraught. In fact, overly so. Caitlyn was eager to know the results of his paternity test. It would mean less to the case if Jim was the father, than if he wasn't. And if someone else was the father, that qualified as a motive for Jim. A crime of passion. Caitlyn wrote Jim's name under Dylan's on the suspect list.

Of course, there was always the possibility that the murderer was a stranger. Either a crazed passerby or someone Wendy knew that no one else was aware of.

Next to draw Caitlyn's perusal was the list of physical evidence. It told a story of Wendy alive until she faced the grave where she would eventually be buried. Her killer shot her in the back of the head. There was no sign of struggle, and as far as she knew, Dr. Kennedy had yet to find any evidence of someone else's DNA under her fingernails or anywhere on her body. The fact that there was no sign of struggle anywhere pointed again to the idea that Wendy knew and trusted her murderer... unless she had been drugged. *Did the coroner's report say there were any drugs in her system?* She'd ask Colt about that tomorrow.

Witnesses from the bar reported seeing both Dylan and Jim talking to Wendy on Friday night. Jim claimed Wendy was with Dylan when he'd last seen her. Dylan claims he never saw Jim and because he left before Wendy did, obviously doesn't have any idea who she talked to after him. Freda, the bartender, agreed they were all three at the bar that night, but noticed nothing unusual about any of them. Nor could she say when they left. The sheriff and Colt were still trying to track down who was at the bar and whether there were any strangers there that evening.

It was going to be a long night waiting until dawn. Tomorrow, Dylan's attorney would arrive and force the sheriff to release him from jail.

15

Caitlyn and Renegade were up early, heading into town to meet the attorney at the Sheriff's Office. She hoped she would be driving Dylan home from jail by noon. The overcast sky added a definite chill to the day, so Caitlyn buttoned her Carhartt jacket and cranked up the heat in the cab. As they pulled to the curb in front of the Sheriff's Office, Caitlyn noticed two other cars parked in front. It seemed the office was already filled with people, so she cracked the windows and left Renegade in the truck. "You stay here, boy. I'll be right back."

Caitlyn pulled open the office door and stepped inside. Sheriff Tackett was behind his desk talking on the phone, and Jim Hague sat in the middle of the room looking flushed and agitated. Mr. and Mrs. Gessler stood behind him, and the poor woman had tucked her hand under her husband's protective arm. Caitlyn scanned the room, her gaze settling on Colt, who leaned against the bars of the small cell in the corner. Behind those same bars stood her brother.

When Colt saw her enter, he walked across the room. "Good morning." He studied her face. Caitlyn wasn't sure what he was looking for. Perhaps encouragement—which he would not get. "Can I take your coat?"

"No thanks, I won't be here that long. I'm just here to meet our attorney and take Dylan home."

The sheriff hung up the phone and addressed Colt. "That was Reed's attorney. He won't be able to make it here this morning, but according to him, we have to let Reed out of the jail."

Caitlyn didn't bother asking the sheriff what the attorney said, she wanted to hear it with her own ears. She pulled out her phone and dialed. After telling the legal office's receptionist who she was and what she was calling for, Caitlyn waited for the lawyer to come on the line. She set her phone on the corner of the sheriff's desk and put it on speaker.

"Good morning, Ms. Reed. I'm glad you called. I just spoke with Sheriff Tackett and explained that I am unable to make it up there this morning. However, I have gone over the details of this case thus far, and have informed the sheriff that he does not have enough probable cause to hold Dylan for questioning any longer. I explained that if he wanted to keep him in jail, he would need to bring him up on formal charges, and the sheriff definitely doesn't have enough evidence to do that. You should be able to pick your brother up this morning and take him home."

"Thank you, Mr. Vanderbilt. I'm standing here in the Sheriff's Office now with you on speakerphone. Others in the office include Deputy-Sheriff Colt Branson, my brother Dylan, Wendy's parents, Mr. and Mrs. Gessler, and Jim Hague, her boyfriend."

Sheriff Tackett crossed his arms and glowered at Caitlyn. "Yes, Mr. Vanderbilt, Sheriff Tackett here. I should inform you that the Gesslers came in this morning to let me know they have appealed to the court for a mandate ordering your client to perform a paternity test. They want to determine whether he is the father of the baby Wendy Gessler was carrying at the time of her death. We have just received news from the lab this morning that Jim Hague, is *not* the father."

Caitlyn bit down hard on her tongue so she wouldn't gasp at the information. She eased up at the coppery tang of blood and glanced at her brother. He looked away.

"Dylan, can you hear me?" The attorney's voice sounded over the line.

Dylan sighed. "Yes, sir. I can hear you fine."

"If the court orders you to take a paternity test, which they may well do considering the circumstances, you will have to comply with that order. Do you understand?"

"Yes, sir." Dylan sat down on the narrow cot, braced his elbows on his knees, and rested his chin in his hand.

The sheriff's mouth pressed into a flat line as he watched Dylan, then he shifted his gaze to Caitlyn. "Since this is a murder case, I expect we will hear from the court by noon."

Caitlyn took a step toward the desk. "We understand the situation. Is there any reason I can't take Dylan home right now and wait to hear from the court there?"

"No reason at all," the attorney answered through the speaker. "Please keep me informed as the day progresses, though I will get a copy of the court order if they send one down."

"I'll call you this afternoon." Caitlyn picked up her phone.

"Very good. Have a nice day."

Caitlyn turned off her phone and slid it into her pocket. She turned to Colt. "It's time for you to release my brother."

Colt nodded, and with the jingle of his keys, walked toward the cell. Caitlyn retrieved Dylan's jacket and cowboy hat from the rack by the door. "Sheriff, my brother didn't kill anyone, though it seems he's all you can focus on. But I'm going to find the real culprit, with or without you. Come on Dylan, let's get you out of here."

Mr. Gessler stepped into Dylan's path and raised his hand to her brother's shoulder. "I hope you understand, Dylan. We've not only lost our daughter, but a grandchild that we'll never know. We're just trying to put the pieces together."

Dylan patted the man's hand and looked him in the eye. "I'm sorry for the loss of your daughter and that you're having to go through all this."

Jim pushed his way into Dylan's face. "I don't know what all was going on between you and Wendy, but if we find out you were the father of that baby, then I guess we'll also know who killed her."

An angry spark flashed in Dylan's eyes, and Caitlyn edged her way between the men. She took Dylan's arm and propelled him toward the door. Brushing past Jim, she said, "Knowing the identity of the baby's father is evidence *only* of paternity, Jim. It does not prove murder. We will not stand for anything less than factual evidence in this case."

As Caitlyn gripped the knob and pulled open the door, the sheriff's desk phone rang. All eyes in the room swung to the device. The sheriff lifted the headset. "Sheriff Tackett's office, this is the sheriff speaking." He nodded several times before answering. "Yes ma'am, I'll look for that fax to come through. Thank you so much for getting right back to me. Time is of the essence in this case. Have a lovely morning." He turned to the Reeds with a self-satisfied grin plastered across his face. "That was the County Clerk calling to inform me that Dylan Reed is required by the court to submit to a paternity test. I guess you two can stop by the clinic on your way home."

Dylan yanked the door out of Caitlyn's hand and stalked out toward her truck. Colt rushed up behind Caitlyn. "I'll walk you out."

Before she left, Caitlyn smiled softly at the Gesslers. "I'll personally let you know what we find out as soon as we know anything. I agree, you have a right to know." Without looking at the sheriff, Caitlyn walked out of the office with Colt following close behind.

Dylan slapped the front fender of Caitlyn's truck and growled his frustration. Renegade responded like a rabid animal from inside the cab, his drooling fangs flashing.

"Dylan, knock it off. Look, you've upset Renegade."

"I'm not getting in the cab with that crazy dog." Dylan leaned against the truck. "You need to teach him some discipline, Caitlyn."

"You're the one who needs some self-discipline," she murmured as she passed her brother. "I'll put him in the bed, but seriously Dylan, you need to stop antagonizing him." Caitlyn went to the driver's side of the truck and opened the door. She clicked Renegade's leash onto his collar and moved him from the cab to the bed of the truck.

Colt opened the passenger side door for Dylan. "It's just a quick DNA cheek swab test. You'll be out of there and home before you know it. I'm sorry about all this, Dylan. I hope you understand, we're just trying to find a killer."

"Yeah, but it isn't me."

"I hope not." Colt stared Dylan down until he turned away and climbed into the truck. He closed the door behind Caitlyn's brother and walked to the tailgate to talk to her. "Hey, I want you to know I thought a lot about our discussion last night. I want to help you as much as I can—without losing my job."

Caitlyn relaxed and warmed with gratitude. "Thank you, Colt."

"I'll call you tonight, after work." His eyes held a promise she didn't want to think about right now.

Caitlyn smiled and climbed into her truck. Colt shut the door behind her, and she started her engine. Though the clinic was only two blocks away, she wasn't about to leave her truck in front of the Sheriff's Office and have to return to it after Dylan took the test. They drove to the clinic in silence.

Caitlyn dropped Dylan at the front door and parked around the corner. She ran Renegade through a few obedience drills while she waited for Dylan outside. Twenty minutes later, her brother emerged from the clinic and without meeting her eye, climbed back into the truck. Caitlyn loaded Renegade back into the bed and told him to lie down. Then together, they set out on the long trek to the Reed family ranch.

"At least you'll get to sleep in your own bed tonight." Caitlyn attempted conversation.

Dylan gazed out the window without saying a word during the drive.

16

Caitlyn's truck bumped to a stop in front of her parents' log cabin home. Their mother rushed out the front door, across the porch, and down the steps before Caitlyn and Dylan got out of the truck.

"Thank heavens you're home, Dylan. I've been so worried about you." Caitlyn's mother embraced her brother.

"I'm fine, mom. I've slept in worse places." He half-heartedly returned her embrace before making his way inside the house.

"Thanks for bringing him home." Her mother met her at the tailgate as she let Renegade out.

"No problem." Caitlyn opened the door to the cab. "Load up, Ren." Renegade leapt into the cab.

"Can't you stay for a while? I thought you might have lunch with us." Her mom hooked her arm through Caitlyn's.

"I guess, but I'll have to leave Ren in the yard. He seems to have issues with Dylan lately, and I don't want anything to happen."

"What do you mean?"

Caitlyn called to Renegade, and the women walked toward the backyard gate.

"I don't know, maybe it's Dylan's nasty attitude. But when he grumbles at me, stomps around, or hits things, Renegade gets upset. I can't blame Ren—he's just being protective." Caitlyn filled a bucket with fresh water and left it for her dog, then followed her mother into the house.

Her mom called out, "John, Dylan, lunch will be ready in the kitchen in ten minutes."

The family gathered, but the mealtime conversation was awkward with everyone trying to ignore the elephant in the room. Eventually, Caitlyn had enough. "So, the Gesslers have appealed to the court and they're forcing Dylan to take a paternity test." Her brother sent her a glare, and she stuck the tip of her tongue out at him.

Their dad bit off an extra-large mouthful of sandwich and took his time chewing, while their mom folded her napkin neatly, pressing creases into the paper with her fingertips. Her worried blue eyes sought Caitlyn. "What does that mean for Dylan's defense?"

"It's just information, Mom. No matter what the results are, it isn't evidence of anything other than whether Dylan was the baby's father, or not. That's it."

"Then why demand the test?" Her mother's gaze was direct.

"I imagine the Gesslers simply want to know. They're grieving and trying to piece this whole thing together. I think the court is showing compassion for them in this terrible time."

"I see." Her mother blinked several times before she shifted her eyes toward Dylan. He shoved his plate away and stood abruptly, having to catch the chair before it toppled over. Saying nothing, he stormed out of the room. Seconds later, they heard the front door slam shut. When her mother turned questioning eyes to Caitlyn, all she could do was shrug. She finished her lunch as calmly as she could, so as not to upset her parents. Then she mumbled a vague excuse before she left to find her brother.

Dylan was out behind the barn, leaning on the fence rail, watching the weanling calves as they bawled for their mothers. She stood next to him and bumped his shoulder with hers. "They're just trying to make sense out of all this."

Dylan spit tobacco juice into the dirt. Chewing was a habit he turned to when something upset him.

Caitlyn stared off into the distance and softened her tone. Not sure she wanted the answer to her question, she pressed on anyway. "What are the test results going to tell us, Dylan?"

He shrugged and sent another brown-tinged stream of spit flying, the sweet scent of wintergreen wafting with it. Footsteps sounded behind them, and Caitlyn turned to see who was coming.

Their dad took a position on Dylan's other side. He leaned backward against the fence, facing them. "Son, I think it's time you came clean about your part in all this. We're going to find out this afternoon that you're the father of that poor baby, aren't we?"

Dylan dug into the dirt with the heel of his boot, but didn't look up at their dad. Finally he answered, "Yes, sir. I believe so."

The impact of his answer was like a sledgehammer to Caitlyn's chest, even though she had suspected it was the truth. "Is that what you and Wendy were talking about at the bar on Friday night?"

"Yeah." Dylan shoved away from the fence and propped his hands on his hips. "She didn't know for sure, but with Hague's test coming back negative, I think she was probably right."

"What the hell, Dylan? You and Wendy?" Heat flooded Caitlyn's face. This looked bad.

Air rushed out of Dylan's lungs, and he shook his head. "The cattle prices had dropped severely in the fall, but I was hopeful they'd pick back up again after the first of the year. The day I saw Wendy, I had just learned that the prices had dropped even farther. That, of course, meant serious reper-cussions for the ranch, so I went and had a few drinks at the Tipsy Cow. Wendy was there, and we got to talking. She and Jim had had a fight, and I don't know—we both ended up getting really drunk. It was stupid, I realize." Dylan faced his father. "I'm sorry, Dad."

Their dad considered Dylan but said nothing. Caitlyn stepped in. "So, last Friday, at the bar, Wendy told you you were the father of her baby?"

"She wasn't sure, but with the timing... She thought I ought to know."

Caitlyn spun away, marched off three paces, turned and stalked back. "And just like that," she snapped her fingers. "You have a motive for murder."

"Your brother didn't kill that girl," her father murmured.

"I'm not saying he did. All I'm saying is, I'm pretty sure the sheriff has enough to arrest Dylan and keep him in jail this time. And you can bet he'll do it." Caitlyn bit down on her lower lip. "What I don't get is that this same information also gives Jim a solid motive—but it doesn't seem like the sheriff's interested in investigating *him*. Good thing *I* am."

"What do you mean, *you* are?" asked her dad.

Caitlyn looked at her father in earnest. "I'm finally putting your investment in my education to good use, Dad. I don't trust Sheriff Tackett to handle this investigation. He's completely blinded by wanting to have a conviction that he's only paying attention to the evidence that supports his preconceived conclusion and discounting everything else. So, I'm running my own investigation, kind of like a private eye."

"You're going to prove Dylan didn't kill Wendy?" Hope floated across her father's expression.

Caitlyn swallowed hard. "I'm working to find out who killed Wendy Gessler. Whoever it was."

Dylan looked at her then, his eyes hard. She stared back until he turned and walked into the barn. "As soon as we receive the results of the test, I'll call the sheriff and tell him he has two solid suspects now, not just one. And Dylan, you need to call Logan. He's the one who recommended the attorney, and he's worried about you."

17

Colt swallowed the last bite of his lunch and was brushing crumbs off his desk, when Sheriff Tackett came through the office door followed by the mayor. He stood as they entered.

"Yes, of course, I'll be running for Sheriff again next term, Mayor." Tackett chuckled and patted the mayor on the back.

As round as he was tall, Mayor Sanders bobbled in behind Tackett. "I was concerned you might want to move back down to Nebraska. We'd hate to lose you."

"Don't you worry about that." The sheriff's smile drooped when he noticed Colt. "I thought I told you to go out to Reed Ranch and confiscate their firearms?"

"Yes, sir. I'm just finishing my lunch break now." In truth, Colt had been dragging his heels. Sheriff Tackett had asked him earlier that morning to collect the guns, but the last thing he wanted to do was to remove all the rifles from his friend's ranch.

Tackett showed the mayor to the chair in front of his desk. "Too worried about filling his belly to drum up any ambition." The sheriff's raspy laugh skidded across Colt's nerves. What did his boss know about his ambitions? Now that he had a couple years of experience, Colt was considering running for Sheriff, too. It wouldn't be hard to do a better job than Tackett, who had only a little more practical experience than he did. Colt lifted his Deputy jacket off the rack and slid it on.

"As soon as you get back here with those guns, I'll call the crime lab and arrange for ballistics testing."

"On my way." Colt left the good ol' boys in the office and drove out toward Reed Ranch. He'd gone about ten miles outside of town, when he saw Caitlyn's truck coming toward him on the other side of the highway. He flashed his lights, signaled, and pulled over to the shoulder of the road.

Caitlyn did the same, then rolled down her window and leaned out. "Where you headed?"

"Out to your parents' place. I thought maybe you'd still be there."

"Why are you going out there?"

"We got some additional information on the case. The lab confirmed the bullet that killed Wendy was a 9mm round. The Sheriff ordered me to confiscate all the guns out at your ranch." The look Caitlyn gave him made Colt squirm with what felt like cold oily eels slithering around in his belly.

"You've got to be kidding me?" Her cheeks flamed. "Do you have a warrant?"

"I do." Colt held up the papers.

"Dylan doesn't even own a 9mm. He has a handgun, but it's a .45."

"Do any of the rifles on the ranch fire 9mm rounds?"

"I'm not sure, but I believe *I'm* the only one in the family who owns a 9mm handgun."

"That might be good news, then. Why don't you pull your truck over to the edge a little farther and leave it here? Come with me back to the ranch?"

"Yeah, okay. I'll come. If only to keep an eye on the situation." Caitlyn gathered her purse and her dog. They darted across the highway and got into his Jeep.

Colt breathed in her fresh lavender scent before he pulled out onto the roadway. "I didn't know you carried a 9mm?"

"Yeah. I have my concealed carry license." Renegade stood in the backseat with his face peering out between them. He panted happily while his eyes shifted back and forth between their conversation. Colt reached up and stroked his muzzle and received a slobbery kiss in return.

"Are you carrying right now?" Colt shot a glance at Caitlyn.

She shook her head and rubbed her palm down her leg. "No, don't worry. There's a gun safe installed in the center console of my truck. I usually keep my gun secured inside there when I'm out and about."

"Why bother with the concealed carry, then? It's not gonna do you much good locked in your truck."

"I take it with me when I think I might need it."

Colt turned onto the ranch drive and meandered up the winding road. When they arrived, John and Dylan were sitting on the front porch drinking a beer.

"Will you open your windows? I need to leave Ren out here. He and Dylan have been irritating each other lately, and I don't want to have to deal with it right now."

Colt tucked that snippet of information away for the time being. As far as he knew, Renegade hadn't always reacted to Dylan aggressively. "Sure." He dropped all four windows down by several inches.

Neither John nor Dylan stood when he and Caitlyn climbed out of the jeep. They made their way over to the bottom of the steps. "Good afternoon, Mr. Reed, Dylan. I'm here because some recent evidence came to light in the

Wendy Gessler case, and the sheriff has ordered me to confiscate all firearms from this property."

Dylan shot to his feet. "Like hell. We can't give you all the guns on the ranch. What happens if a pack of wolves or a mountain lion comes down and attacks my herd? We have to be able to defend our livelihood."

"I understand your concern, Dylan, but I have a warrant and I have to follow orders. The sheriff told me to come and collect all your firearms, so that's what I've got to do."

"Yeah, well, the sheriff is an idiot. He knows nothing about running a ranch."

Colt placed a boot on the second step and leaned forward on his knee. "I understand where you're coming from, Dylan, and I'll return your guns as soon as possible. We just need to run them through ballistics."

Caitlyn ran past Colt up the steps and turned at the top to glower down at him. "You told me the killer shot Wendy with a 9mm. Why then, do you need all the guns? That makes no sense. I can't believe you found a judge who would issue such a warrant."

Colt glanced away and released a pent-up breath. He hated having to be the one upsetting Caitlyn's family. Turning back to face Caitlyn, he nodded. "I'm surprised by the warrant too." In fact, it had stunned him until he remembered the "good old boys' club" that the sheriff was a part of and knew it hadn't been hard for him to convince his lifelong pal, the judge, to issue the request. "But Judge Merrick wrote it up. Tackett believes that if Dylan is the perpetrator, he could be a threat to society. Therefore, he ordered the confiscation of all firearms from the premises." Colt shifted his gaze to Dylan. "I'm sorry about this. Hopefully, it will all be over soon."

John rose to his feet. "Well then, Deputy, I guess you better come in and start collecting. Dylan, you best go get your .45." Dylan stormed into the house. Caitlyn followed him, but John focused on Colt. "Do *you* think my son killed that girl?"

Colt held the older man's gaze and swallowed. "It's a possibility, sir. I'm doing everything I can to find out what happened that night. The truth will win out, one way or the other." John nodded and turned to go inside, leaving Colt to follow behind. Caitlyn led him to the gun safe in her father's office where Dylan removed the rifles, one at a time. He opened each barrel to show Colt the guns were unloaded. There were six rifles total, along with Dylan's handgun. Caitlyn videotaped the entire confiscation on her phone. She also documented each gun by its serial number. Colt, Dylan, and John carried the firearms out to the deputy's Jeep, followed by Caitlyn and her video camera.

Colt secured the weapons, then turned to Caitlyn. "Your 9mm isn't here, is it?"

"No, like I told you, it's locked up in my truck."

"Fine, will you give it to me when I drive you back there?" Colt laid the rifles carefully on a blanket in the back of his Jeep.

"Why do you want *my* gun? Am I a suspect now, too?" Caitlyn crossed her arms in a huff.

"No, but we'll need to have it tested, anyway. It won't be a problem to get a separate warrant if you want me to." Colt closed the hatch of his SUV.

"Damn straight I do. You can't just take my gun!"

Colt clenched his jaw to keep from saying anything that would make Caitlyn angrier and made his way over to John and Dylan. He stuck out his hand and shook John's, then offered it to Dylan.

Dylan stared at his outstretched hand for a moment before he gripped it hard. "Take good care of my rifles. We need them back as soon as possible."

Colt nodded and turned to leave. He and Caitlyn got into the Jeep, and Caitlyn checked if Ren was doing all right. He seemed to sense her agitation, and he licked her face. They made their way back down to the highway and her truck. During the drive, both he and Caitlyn chose the company of their own thoughts.

Eventually, Colt spoke. "Something interesting happened today." He waited for Caitlyn to look at him. "After you and Dylan left the Sheriff's Office, Tackett told the Gesslers and Hague that Wendy died from a gunshot wound to the head."

Compassion filled Caitlyn's eyes. "How awful for the Gesslers. She was their only child."

"Yeah, the information upset them, but Jim started rambling on about how Wendy had mentioned wanting to disappear. He said that he worried she was going to kill herself, and now that he knows she was pregnant with Dylan's baby, he could understand why."

"He doesn't know for sure who the father was, and why didn't he say something about her suicidal thoughts before now?"

"I asked him that same thing. He claims it was because he wished to honor her by keeping her secret. Jim admitted Wendy had asked him to take her to Sundance on Friday night after they left the bar. He said he dropped her off at a motel where she wanted to spend the weekend thinking."

"So, now he admits he was the last one to see Wendy? His story changes with the wind. And what kind of idiot would leave someone who is admittedly suicidal alone in a motel?" Caitlyn searched Colt's face. "Do you believe him?"

"I don't know."

"Is he trying to say that Wendy killed herself?"

"I think that's what he was implying."

"But she couldn't have. You told me the killer shot her in

the back of the head. Not to mention, someone buried her body."

Colt raised his eyebrows at the discrepancy. "I know, right? And I learned another crucial piece of information today. Wendy's postmortem toxicology report came in. Doc Kennedy found Rohypnol in her system."

Caitlyn scrunched her brows and sat deep in silence, mulling over the new findings for several moments before she spoke. "I suppose she could have taken the drug herself if she wanted to commit suicide, but Rohypnol doesn't seem like the best drug of choice for that purpose. We're left to wonder, did Wendy drug herself, which is highly doubtful, or was she drugged by someone else? How did Wendy end up on the ridge at Reed Ranch? Who was with her? And where were Jim and Dylan in the hours after ten o'clock that night?"

They pulled up behind Caitlyn's truck and Colt shut off his engine. He turned in his seat to face her. "What does your gut tell you? Do you believe Dylan could have murdered Wendy?"

Caitlyn slowly swiveled her head back and forth. "I can't imagine it. But I want to know the truth no matter what." She pulled on her lip with her teeth and cocked her head at Colt. "This thing with Jim makes no sense. Does it?"

Colt agreed. "We need to keep searching. I've been investigating the guy's past, but I haven't found much to go on yet. Don't worry though, I'll keep digging—we'll find the truth."

18

Caitlyn opened the door for Renegade, who hopped out and ran toward the truck. The bed listed to the left and as she approached, she realized why. "You've got to be kidding."

"What's wrong?" Colt was right behind her.

"Look." She pointed at her back wheel. "Someone slit my tire. Damn it! Truck tires are expensive." Caitlin jerked away and went to get the jack from its place behind the seat.

Colt squatted down and ran his fingers over the five-inch cut. "Yep, definitely done on purpose."

Caitlin stomped back. "Who would do something like this? Seriously. Who would take the time to stop, get out, vandalize a truck tire, and then drive away?"

"Kids, most likely. Daring each other into doing stupid shit." Colt took the jack from her. "Here, let me."

Together, they made quick work of changing her tire. "Thanks for your help." Caitlyn took the lug wrench from him.

"No problem." He followed her to her cab. "Do you think

I can get your gun now, Catie? And I'd like to see your safe."
He peered into the truck over her shoulder.

"I don't have to give you my gun without a warrant, and
you know it." She had nothing to hide, but that wasn't the
point.

"You're right, but I also know it will only take a phone call
from the sheriff to his good buddy, the judge. He'll have that
warrant in a flash and then we'll be right back where we
started."

"This sucks."

"I know, but when they find nothing, it will clear
things up."

She rolled her eyes before clicking open the center
console and pressed a combination code into the keypad on
the black safe. The lock mechanism clicked and released. She
opened the lid and lifted her pistol out. After releasing the
magazine, Caitlyn removed the bullet she kept in the
chamber before she handed the empty firearm over to Colt.
"Here you go. How long do you think you'll need to have
this?"

"I'll ask them to rush the test through, but it depends on
how backed up they are." Colt took the gun and held his
hand out for her magazine. "Can you account for this gun's
whereabouts all of last Friday night?"

Caitlyn thought about it, and her chest compressed. She
wished she had a concrete answer. "I know where I kept it
the whole time, but I didn't have it on me. I left it locked
inside the truck while I had dinner at my parents' house that
evening."

"Was Dylan there for dinner?"

"Yes, but he left before I did."

"And was your gun in the console when you got home
that night?"

An unwelcome chill coursed through Caitlyn's body, and

her eyes flew to meet Colt's. "To be perfectly honest, I don't know for sure, though I can be reasonably certain it was. The thing is, I didn't bring my gun into my house with me when I got home. Usually I do, but it was late, and I was carrying a bunch of leftovers from my mom." Caitlyn chewed on her lip, remembering the events that took place. "It was there in the morning, though. I am certain of that."

"I'm sure there's nothing to worry about, then. Does Dylan know your combination?"

"No. The only other person who has my combo is my dad."

"Does he have it written somewhere?"

The back of Caitlyn's neck prickled. "I don't know."

"I'm sure it will be fine. We'll run the ballistics, and I'll have your gun back to you in no time." Colt took her Glock to his Jeep and Caitlyn videoed the exchange. He turned before he got into the car. "Are you doing anything later?"

"Just going over this case."

"Want company?" Colt's car radio squawked, and the Sheriff's voice crackled over the line. "Deputy Branson, this is Sheriff Tackett. Do you copy?"

Colt reached in, unhooked the transmitter, and pressed the button. "Loud and clear."

"What's your 10-20?"

"I'm about ten miles from Moose Creek on the forest highway. I have Caitlyn Reed with me, and we're completing the transfer of firearms."

"That's fortuitous. Bring Ms. Reed back to the office with you. We can check the firearms into evidence together."

Caitlyn gave Colt a thumbs up. "Good idea. Tell Sheriff Tackett I'd like to have an official receipt, signed by him for all the guns."

Colt relayed her message.

"Of course." Tackett's voice crackled. "Explain to Ms.

Reed, that I always do everything by the book." Colt smirked and rolled his eyes. "Yes, sir. Out." He clicked the radio off.

Caitlyn shook her head and canted it toward town. "Renegade and I will follow you."

"Sounds good. Maybe you'll let me buy you a cup of coffee afterwards?"

"We'll see." Caitlyn and Renegade climbed into the truck and tailed Colt back to the Sheriff's office. She had to admit to herself that she enjoyed spending time with Colt, as much as she ever did. And that smile... she found herself teasing him just to see if she could get him to flash it at her. It was the learning to trust him again that was hard.

At the Sheriff's Office, they carried the firearms into the building. Catie videotaped while Colt and the sheriff tagged each firearm and documented it on an evidence form. "How long will it take to run these guns through ballistics, Sheriff?" she asked.

"I'll let you know when it's done."

Caitlyn sat on the edge of his desk. "Tell me, what do you make out of Jim Hague revealing that Wendy was suicidal?"

The Sheriff's eyes popped open before they narrowed to slits and aimed their anger at Colt. "Talking out of school, are we?" The sheriff pointed and shook his beefy finger at Caitlyn. "You need to keep your nose out of this investigation."

A low rumble echoed in Renegade's chest, and he took a menacing step into the space between Caitlyn and the sheriff. Caitlyn reached down and stroked his head. "I will *not* stay away from this investigation. My degree is in criminal justice, and I intend to use what I've learned. I'm confident I can do a better job than you're doing."

Sheriff Tackett edged toward Caitlyn, and Renegade's growl rolled into a bark. He bared his teeth, and Tackett retreated behind his desk. "You've got your receipt, now get your mangy dog out of my office. I don't care what you studied in school. By the way, do you have a private investigator's license? Because if you don't, I can bring you up on charges for interfering with an ongoing investigation."

The sheriff's bluster, no matter how puffed up he got, didn't intimidate Caitlyn. "Sheriff, the problem is that you've already decided Dylan's guilty. Now you're only looking for evidence that will prove your assumption. Don't neglect the evidence that points in a different direction."

"Like what?" Tackett scoffed.

"I know you want to believe that if Dylan is the baby's father, it gives him a motive for murder. You're guessing that maybe Wendy refused to have an abortion, and so Dylan killed her. Is that your line of thinking?"

The sheriff lowered himself into his desk chair, crossed his arms over his belly, and nodded. "There's probably more to it, but that's the long and short of it."

"Right. To my point—you're completely neglecting the fact that Jim would then also have a motive for murder. After all, another man slept with his girlfriend. Jealousy can definitely incite a crime of passion. And that type of motive holds far more water than the one you're assigning to Dylan. Not to mention, Hague lied when he said Dylan was the last one seen talking to Wendy before she disappeared."

"I understand your position, but love for your brother clouds your perspective." Sheriff Tackett leaned forward, his face pinched in anger. "Now I'm warning you, stay out of this case. Let the professionals handle it."

"Ha! I'd like to know what makes you a professional, Sheriff Tackett? Somehow, the people of Moose Creek elected you to this office, even though you didn't live here and barely passed the Law Enforcement Academy exams." Caitlyn reached down and smoothed Renegade's hackles. "At least I can rely on Colt. Come on Ren, we're out of here."

19

Caitlyn ended up not only having coffee with Colt, but dinner as well. By the time she left town, it was almost ten o'clock. The late hour surprised her when she looked at her watch. Their time together was engaging, and she had more fun than she expected. Maybe she could finally move past her anger toward him. At least he stuck up for her desire to run her own investigation. Sheriff Tackett, on the other hand, had been so angry about it, he'd even threatened to bring her up on charges.

Colt walked her to her truck. She lingered at the door, waiting to see if maybe he'd try to kiss her again, but he shoved his hands in his pockets and said goodnight. Feeling vaguely let down, she scoffed at herself. *What? You wanted him to kiss you after you sent him packing last night? Stupid move.*

Renegade leapt into the cab and Caitlyn heard paper crumple. She reached for the loose sheet lying on her seat. Someone had marked it in red letters. "Mind your own damn business, bitch — or else you'll be next!" A thousand pins pricked her skin. She looked for Colt, but he had gone. *Who would have left this?* The note rattled her even though she had

Renegade with her. Caitlyn glanced in the bed of her truck, then jumped into her cab and locked the doors. Her hand shook as she slid her keys into the ignition. The skin on the back of her neck puckered, and she wondered if the person who left her the threat was watching her from the shadows. *I should have kept my gun.*

Shaky and deep in thought, Caitlyn made her way down the highway. Keeping an eye on the rearview mirror, she sifted through what she knew about the murder case so far. She desperately wanted to believe Dylan, but there was a chunk of time he had yet to account for that Saturday night. *Had he gone to the motel after Jim dropped Wendy off? And if so, why? How would he have known she was there?* She wished she could get ahold of Wendy's phone records. Caitlyn chewed on her lower lip. *Could Dylan have written the threatening note?*

Renegade snuggled next to her, his head on her lap. He was sound asleep, but his legs were moving. She smiled at her friend, who was clearly chasing something in his dreams. "I hope you catch it, boy. Whatever you're after."

By the time Caitlyn turned onto the road that led to her cabin, she had calmed down. Fatigue crept its way up her neck and her eyelids were heavy. She was far more tired than she had realized and was glad to be home. The image of Colt's rugged grin when he'd said good night flashed across her mind, and her body responded with a flush of warmth. It would be nice if her body and her mind could get on the same page.

She parked her truck in front of her cabin and gently woke Renegade. He stretched his way into a seated position and indulged in a wide-mouthed yawn. "Come on, sleepyhead, let's get you to bed." Caitlyn opened her door and stepped to the ground. Renegade hopped out after her. He darted off to do his business, and Caitlyn let herself inside. She reached for the light switch, but the bulb didn't turn on.

"Damn." Caitlyn felt her way through the living room to the lamp by the sofa and turned its knob. Click. Nothing.

Caitlyn groaned and inched across the dark room to the kitchen drawer where she kept her flashlight. Snapping it on, the instant strong, bright beam gave her relief. Full batteries. Now, to remember where the breaker box was. Caitlyn had lived in the cabin for less than a year and had never needed the breakers.

She flashed the light on the kitchen walls and found nothing. She didn't think it was in the living room, so she made her way to her bedroom. The box wasn't there either, so she opened the linen closet. The door creaked and Caitlyn made a mental note to spray the hinges with WD-40. She splashed the beam on the walls and ceiling, but no box. Turning back, she passed the door to her tiny bathroom. Out of nowhere, blinding pain shot through her skull. Bright white lights glimmered behind her eyelids as her lungs sucked in a great gasp of air. Her hand flew to the point of impact but never made it there. Gloved fingers gripped her wrist. A powerful arm flew around her chest, pulling her backward into the thick body of a man who stood much taller than she. His hand clapped over her mouth before she could gather a scream. Caitlyn scrunched her eyes at the pain radiating through her head and tried to think. She fought against the man's arms and bit his hand, but he held her fast.

Her pulse rocketed, her heart demanding oxygen her lungs could not provide. She jerked her head up and sucked air in through her nose. Lifting her boot, she kicked into the man's shin and scraped the edge of her heel down to his ankle where she stomped. The man growled and twisted her head around. Caitlyn feared he would break her neck.

The intruder whispered into her ear with hot, rancid breath. "You should've minded your own business. Now look what you're making me do. This is your own fault."

With all of her strength, Catie bucked against the man. She threw her head back into his chin. But that only hurt her worse. Renegade barked furiously outside, scratching and clawing at the front door. If only she had let him in before she went to find the flashlight. The prowler must've been hiding in her cabin, waiting for her to come home. She grunted in her effort to get loose. There was no one to hear her scream way out here, so she conserved her breath. With her free hand, she clawed at the fingers covering her mouth. She pried the man's thumb out and yanked down as hard as she could. In response, he shoved her forcefully, face-first against the wall, bracing his forearm against the back of her neck. Her cheek bone scraped against the log wall. He twisted her left arm around behind her and forced it up past her shoulder blade. Caitlyn cried out in pain. Another inch and her arm would snap. Renegade went crazy outside. He sounded like an entire pack of wild dogs.

The man chuckled. "A lot of good your dog's doing you out there."

"You have to leave the cabin sometime," Caitlyn choked before she sucked in more air. "And when you do, he'll tear you apart." Caitlyn forced a bravado she didn't feel into her voice.

"Not if he's dead."

Caitlyn's heart shrank into a tiny fist, its rapid beats each aching with agony. There was nothing she could do to save herself or her dog.

Glass shattered in the living room. From the darkness of night, Renegade shot through the plate-glass window. Shards, glittering in the flashlight's beam, sprayed around the room. In a flash, her dog sprang on the man, his fangs tearing into his biceps. The attacker screamed at the torment of his shredded flesh. He wielded his gun as a club and spun to defend himself against the wolf-like teeth. When he raised his arm, the butt of the pistol cracked Caitlyn in the temple and she dropped to her knees, fighting for consciousness.

The man swung his weapon again and slammed it against Renegade's skull, two, three, four times. Her sweet dog yelped with each blow. It wasn't until the fifth strike that he released his hold. He opened his jaws and fell to the floor.

"Renegade!" screamed Caitlyn. Or she thought she screamed, but she couldn't open her mouth. Heavy footsteps retreated, and the backdoor slammed. An engine roared away. *Thank God. He must have thought we were both dead.* She needed to get to Renegade. Caitlyn tried her voice again. Words sprang to her lips, but only muffled whimpers sounded from them. She drifted, wrestling with the shadows that snaked across her mind.

Later, Caitlyn came to with no idea how long she'd been out. She pushed herself up from the floor to her knees. The searing pain in her head pulsed, causing her to throw up on the carpet. She took shallow breaths and forced her eyes to open. *Renegade.*

The beautiful body of her dog, her best friend, lay lifeless at the edge of the living room carpet in the center of a pool of broken glass. A sob tore from Caitlyn's throat as she crawled forward. She reached out her bruised arm, and though it felt like a searing blade pierced her forearm, she rested her hand on the side of Renegade's face. "Oh, Ren, I'm so sorry," she cried.

A soft whimper echoed from inside Renegade's throat. Burning tears washed through Caitlyn's eyes. She scooted closer to her dog. "Renegade? Are you okay, boy?" She stroked his face, and he opened his eyes. Moonlight reflected in his dilated pupils that spoke of great pain. Her head was too heavy for her to hold any longer, and she rested it on the carpet next to him. "You're going to be okay, boy. I've got you now," she whispered as she floated off on dark clouds.

Caitlyn jerked awake again, sometime later. She licked her dry lips and tasted blood. With her fingers, she prodded her back jeans pocket for her phone. It was still there and hopefully hadn't been destroyed in the attack. She pulled out the device and saw a spiderweb of fractured glass on the screen. "No, no, no." Pushing the button to turn it on, she pressed the numbers and dialed 911. Relief washed over her when the voice of a woman at the county dispatch answered. Caitlyn explained as quickly and clearly as she could manage that an intruder had attacked her in her home. "Please send help, right away."

"Do you need medical attention?"

"No. I think I'll be fine. Just send a sheriff." Caitlyn curled up next to Renegade to wait and drifted once again away from her pain.

20

Colt received the call from the dispatcher, immediately recognized Caitlyn's address, and responded he was on his way. He'd been on his nightly patrol through Moose Creek and the nearby ranches, and was driving in the opposite direction, when he clicked on his lights and siren. In the middle of the highway, he spun the wheel, and making a U-turn, he flooded his turbocharged engine with fuel. He barreled through the night toward Caitlyn's place. Each mile seemed a light year until he came to a skidding halt in her yard.

The predawn sky was brightening, and he noticed at once the smashed-in picture window. There were no lights on in or around the cabin, and an icy dread clawed at his chest. As he jumped out of the Jeep, he unholstered his gun and held it with both hands in firing position. He crept toward the front door. The splintered shards from the window fell inward. The intruder must've thrown something through the plate glass to gain entry. Colt approached the edge of the window casing and peered into the cabin. The interior was too dark for him to see anything, except for a lone flashlight beam glowing from its spot on the floor.

Fearing the intruder was still there, as quietly as he could, Colt continued to the front entrance. Wrapping his fingers around the knob, he slowly turned. It was unlocked. Holding a small Maglite on the top of his gun, Colt eased the door open and panned the room. Caitlyn was there, sprawled on the floor next to her equally still dog. Her long dark hair cascaded over splintered shards of glass. "Catie!" he whispered harshly. He flashed his light throughout the great room. No one else was there. He rushed to her and crouched down to feel for a pulse in her neck. A weak bump pressed against his fingertips. She was alive! *Thank, God!*

His training insisted he clear the house to be sure they were no longer in danger before he did more for Caitlyn, but it killed him to leave her lying injured and unconscious— helpless on the floor. He sped through the cabin, clearing the bathroom and Caitlyn's bedroom. There was no sign of anyone. Certain the intruder was gone, Colt ran to Caitlyn. Gently, he rolled her to her back, checking her for wounds. It appeared she was bleeding only from her head, which was bad enough. He patted her cheek. "Catie? It's me, Colt. You're safe, honey. Can you wake up for me?"

A weak groan spilled from Caitlyn's mouth. Her eyes flickered. She stared unseeing for a few seconds before her vision focused on him. "Colt?" She strained to sit up.

"Don't try to move. I'm calling an ambulance."

"No. I'm fine… Renegade." The four words seemed to wear her out.

Colt reached for her dog's neck. Assuming that's where he would look for a pulse in a dog, he dug his fingers into Renegade's fur. He didn't find a pulse, but he could feel the dog breathing. "Renegade's here, right next to you, Catie.

He's alive. You're both going to be fine." He didn't have the right to make that promise. But he said it anyway.

"Water?"

"Sure, let me get you some." Colt jumped to his feet and attempted to turn on the kitchen light. When it didn't respond, a puzzle piece fell into place. He had been to a lot of these small cabins and knew the breaker box was usually on the back porch. Colt made his way outside and found what he expected. Someone had switched off the electricity. No surprise there. He flipped on the lever, and light flooded the tiny cabin. On his way back to Caitlyn, he filled a glass with water.

Kneeling beside her, Colt helped her sit up enough to take a small drink. "You have a head injury. Are you hurt anywhere else?"

"Just scrapes and bruises, I think."

"Do you know who did this to you?"

"No. I never saw his face." Caitlyn scrunched her eyes against the pain and a tear pushed out the corner of one eye and tracked down her bloodied cheek.

"Whoever it was, left you both for dead."

Caitlyn's head barely bobbed in agreement. "We need to help Ren. Call the emergency vet number." She opened her eyes and turned her head. Colt followed her gaze to the refrigerator. The vet's magnetized business card was the only thing stuck to the front of the appliance. Colt laid her head softly on the carpet and went to get the number. He made the call and described what he could of Renegade's injuries. Then he told the vet he'd bring the dog in as soon as possible.

By the time he finished speaking to Dr. Moore, Caitlyn had climbed to her feet. She was testing out her limbs when she clutched her forearm. "Ah!"

Colt rushed to her side. It gutted him to see her in such pain with dried blood on her face and in her hair. "I'm calling

133

an ambulance, whether or not you want one. They can take care of you while I drive Renegade to the vet. You need to sit down. I'll call the sheriff and he can start an investigation." Seeing Caitlyn weak and vulnerable, knowing she could have been killed, stirred a feral sort of protectiveness in him. He didn't want to leave her side, but Renegade needed emergency care too. At least that was something Colt could do for the brave woman he held in his arms.

Caitlyn protested, but he dialed the paramedics, anyway. Helpless to do anything more, he started a pot of coffee. Caitlyn refused to leave Renegade's side, so he brought her a steaming mug when it was ready. The sun seeped into the morning and warmed the day.

"Help will be here soon. How's Ren doing?" Caitlyn's dog lay propped on his forelegs and he raised his head. His ears perked straight up, though blood caked his fur. "He looks like he's feeling a little better, anyway." Colt stroked the dog's battered head and checked over the rest of Renegade's body the best he could. The fur on his head was sticky and matted with blood, the same red glistened at the side of his mouth. Slivers of glass pierced his paws. "Poor guy. I'll have you taken care of as soon as they come to get your mom." Renegade whined in response. "I called the sheriff. He wasn't in the office yet, so I asked dispatch to tell him to meet me here. He should be here soon." Minutes later tires sounded on the gravel drive.

Sheriff Tackett knocked once on the already open door. "What happened here?" he said speculatively as he scanned the destruction. He stepped into the room, adjusting his jacket, and Colt stood. "Are you all right, Ms. Reed?"

"An intruder was hiding inside Caitlyn's house when she got home last night, and he attacked her. Renegade was outside, and he broke in through the window to protect her. An ambulance is on the way. As soon as it gets here, I'm taking Catie's dog to the vet. Then I'll come back here to help you investigate the crime."

The sheriff ran a hand down the length of his face. "I'm still in charge around here, Deputy."

Colt ground his teeth and looked away so Tackett couldn't see his irritation.

"No matter. Sounds like a good plan, except for one thing. I'll be following the ambulance to the clinic, because as soon as Ms. Reed is well enough to leave there, I'll be taking her to the jail." The sheriff shifted to a wide leg stance. He crossed his arms, grimaced, and slid his hands to his hips instead.

21

"What?" Caitlyn and Colt shouted together.

"What are you talking about, Sheriff?" Caitlyn limped one step toward him. Her body was on fire.

"I got the preliminary ballistics reports back and they show the bullet that killed Wendy definitely came from a 9mm *pistol*, and the casing found at the scene has a partial print on it. I'm betting it's yours. I need to take you in for questioning and to get your fingerprints. I think this additional evidence explains why you've been sticking your nose into this investigation. You've been hoping to distract us from the truth. Right now, I want to figure out if you were trying to frame your brother, or if you're in cahoots with him."

Caitlyn felt as though someone had run her over with a semi, and Colt looked the same. He gaped at her. "Catie?"

"That's not possible, Sheriff." She turned to Colt and held out her uninjured arm in a plea for understanding. "You don't believe this, do you?"

"That report comes from the crime lab, Caitlyn. It's not

just the Sheriff's opinion." Colt's face paled under his dark blond morning whiskers, and he dropped his gaze to the floor. He swallowed several times, looking as though he might be sick. Escaping into the bedroom, he returned with a blanket. He unfolded it next to Renegade and carefully scooted Caitlyn's dog onto it. Colt lifted Renegade in his arms. "He's lighter than I expected," he said as he carried the dog to the door.

"Wait!" Caitlyn stroked Renegade's face and kissed his nose. A wave of dizziness overwhelmed her senses, and she grasped onto Colt as she looked up at him. "I didn't kill Wendy. You have to believe me."

"Did Dylan do this to you?" He looked deep into her eyes. "Was he the one who attacked you?"

Shocked that he'd think so, Caitlyn couldn't answer. Colt pulled away and crossed the porch to the stairs.

"Someone left a threatening note in my truck last night while we were at dinner." She called after him. "Think, Colt! There's more to all of this than meets the eye."

He glanced back at her, nodded once, and started down the steps. He didn't get far before Renegade wriggled loose from his hold. The dog leapt to the ground and yelped when he landed on his splinter filled paws.

"Ren!" Caitlyn dashed toward him, though a wave of vertigo overcame her.

Sheriff Tackett held her back, sending Renegade into a fury. Even through his pain, Caitlyn's dog fought to defend her. The poor guy didn't understand. He snarled as Tackett grabbed hold of her and she winced in pain.

"Easy Sheriff. Her arm is injured." Colt warned before he crouched down. "It's okay, Ren. I'm just trying to help you." Renegade snapped at him. "Whoa!" Colt jumped away. "He's never done that before."

"You've never stood by when someone manhandled me before, either." Caitlyn glared at him.

"Tell him to back off, or we'll have to call animal control," Colt pleaded. "I need to get him to the vet."

The sheriff held his phone in the air. "Already did. We can't have a dangerous dog hampering us from doing our jobs."

CAITLYN SOOTHED Renegade with her voice while Colt stood back. He tried to reconcile what she'd told him with the sheriff's evidence. Just yesterday, she assured him she'd locked her gun in the truck safe—that it was there all day and night last Saturday. *She lied to me. Catie and Dylan are tangled up in this murder somehow.* His mind reeled at the thought. *How could I have been so naïve?* Caitlyn had used his feelings for her against him. Colt shook his head and stared off into the forest, grappling with his emotions.

Before long, the county's animal control vehicle rolled to a stop before them. The driver got out and unclipped a six-foot pole with a loop of rope on the end from the side of the truck. "This the nuisance dog?" He pointed the device at Renegade.

"Please, be careful. He's hurt," Caitlyn cried.

The man scratched his chin. "Probably why he's trying to bite." He reached the post near Renegade and fed more line through the hollow pole into the rope loop. He slipped it over the dog's head and tightened. Renegade went crazy. Ignoring the pain he must have felt in his paws and head, he shook his body back and forth, growling and gnashing his fangs. He caught hold of the aluminum post and crushed it in his fierce jaws.

"Stop! Stop it!" Caitlyn surged toward the man. Tackett held her back.

The animal control officer dropped the post and darted to his truck. When he returned, he held a rifle. He aimed and fired. Renegade stumbled before falling to the dirt. Caitlyn screamed, and every muscle in Colt's body flexed.

The man thrust his hand out as if to stop Caitlyn from attacking him. "It's okay, ma'am. That was just a tranquilizer dart. This way he won't hurt himself, or me." He glanced at Colt. "Help me get the dog into the truck, then you can follow me to the vet." The man approached Caitlyn's dog and slipped a muzzle over his head, buckling it on the last notch.

Colt's throat was tight, and his stomach had turned to stone. Everything about this morning was awful. He helped carry a limp Renegade to the cage in the man's truck, but before he locked the door, Colt loosened the muzzle. He got into his Jeep and called to Caitlyn through his window. "I'll see you at the jail as soon as I have anything to report on Renegade."

Long strands of hair hung across her bruised face, and her eyes were wild. "Colt—" she called.

He couldn't bear to hear the rest, so he gunned his engine and rolled up the glass as he drove away. Colt forced himself to breathe. Forced himself to drive to town and not turn around. He had to have some space to think about the insane turn of events.

Colt passed the ambulance, turning down Caitlyn's road, as he followed the animal control officer into Moose Creek. They drove directly to the clinic where they met the veterinarian, Dr. Moore, in the parking lot.

The control officer opened the doors where a muzzled Renegade slept. "This dog is nuts, Doc. I slipped my tomahawk pole over his neck, and he went ballistic. Look what he did to my catching rod." The man pointed to the twisted and dented aluminum. "I tried twice before I had to trank him to get him into the truck."

Dr. Moore unlatched the cage and ran gentle fingers over Renegade's face and ears, pausing near the bleeding wounds. "I understand, but I must say for future reference, the worst thing you could do to a dog with a head injury is tranquilize him. How long will the drug last?"

Colt swallowed the emotions that threatened to overwhelm him. He felt especially bad for Renegade, who was only trying to protect Caitlyn. Then, of course, there was Caitlyn—he couldn't think about her right now. The sense of betrayal he grappled with was dark and heavy. "Here, let me help you, Doc." He reached for the dog.

"Hold on, I'm going to get a cart from my office. I'd like the transfer to be as gentle as possible." The doctor went inside the clinic.

The animal control officer leaned against the side of his truck and lit a cigarette. "I know what the vet says, but I had to trank him. You saw—you were there."

"Seems like we should've tried to calm him down. He was spooled up because the sheriff was holding Caitlyn back. She could've calmed him down if we'd have let her." Colt clenched his fists. Anger coursed through him, directed at the sheriff for his rough handling of Caitlyn, the control officer for the way he had treated Renegade, and the intruder who had hurt them both. "As soon as we get him on the cart, you can leave."

"I'll need to perform an aggressive dog evaluation when the doctor releases him from the vet clinic."

"The dog is injured. Of course, he's aggressive. That seems natural to me. I'll take it from here." Colt didn't want the control officer anywhere near Renegade.

The vet returned with a rolling cart, and together he and Colt gently lifted Renegade out of the truck and laid him on the stainless steel. They rolled him inside, and Colt assisted the vet in cleaning Renegade up and prepping him for the glass removal from his paws.

Dr. Moore considered Colt over the top of his glasses. "So, you don't think this dog has aggression issues?"

"No. Not unless he feels like his owner is in danger. Then, he gets aggressive pretty quick." Colt ran his hand down the length of Renegade's side.

"I agree. Caitlyn has been consistent in bringing him in for his regular shots and exams since he was a puppy. He's always been well behaved when I've seen him. He seems to socialize nicely around other dogs that are here when he comes in, too."

"Renegade probably saved Caitlyn's life last night. An intruder attacked her in her home. Renegade crashed through the living room window in order to save her. That's where the glass in his paws is from. She's on her way now to the clinic to get checked out, too."

Concern washed over the doctor's face. "Will she be all right?"

"I hope so." Lumps of lead collided in Colt's stomach.

The vet nodded. "Sounds like Renegade is a perfect dog for a single woman living on her own."

"Absolutely. I just wish we caught the attacker. Renegade tore into him to get him off of Caitlyn. I imagine he got some good bites in before the man knocked him out. I'll be on the lookout for any injured men around town."

"So, you think the attacker was a local man?"

"I have no real way of knowing, but Caitlyn didn't think he stole anything. It may have been a personal attack rather than a robbery."

"Was she hurt badly?" Dr. Moore peered up at him through steel-frame glasses.

"When I found her, her head was bleeding. The guy had

knocked her unconscious. She seemed lucid when she came to, but her arm was hurting. The doctor at the clinic will let us know the extent of her injuries."

"Thank God it wasn't worse than that. He could have killed her." The doctor frowned. "Thanks for your help bringing Renegade in, but I've got it from here. Sounds like you have a job to do. I'll take him back, get some x-rays, and begin removing the glass splinters. Shall I call you, or Caitlyn, when he wakes up?" The vet pulled the cart toward the door to the procedure room.

Colt wasn't about to tell him that Caitlyn would be at the jail. "Why don't you call my number and I'll let Caitlyn know? I'm not sure how long she'll be at the clinic."

"Of course, Deputy. I hope she's okay. Tell her she can call me if she has any questions."

"Thanks, Doc. I'll be looking for your call." Colt shook the man's hand and left the vet clinic. He prayed Caitlyn's head was going to be okay. He had heard nothing since he drove away from her cabin, so he went back to his Jeep and radioed the sheriff. "Are you still at the hospital with Caitlyn?"

"The doctor patched Ms. Reed up and gave her the all clear to leave the hospital. We are on our way to the jail, now. You can meet us there." The sheriff sounded pleased about the situation.

Colt's shoulders relaxed a little, hearing that Caitlyn was well enough to be released. On his way to the Sheriff's office, he stopped by the café and picked up some fresh-baked, gooey, cinnamon rolls and two dark-roast coffees to go. He and Caitlyn hadn't had breakfast, and he figured she was probably as starving as he was. His naturally warm thoughts of Caitlyn turned cold as he remembered why Tackett took her into custody. *Could she possibly be a murderer? Dylan's accomplice? Maybe she's involved in some other way? Had she really been using me all along?* His stomach churned and a

not to worry that she had no alibi for the time of the murder. She'd been driving home—alone—in her truck and had seen no one after she left her parents' house that Friday night until Sunday morning. She'd spent Saturday home alone, doing chores and working on her property. The only one who could corroborate her whereabouts was Renegade.

"Sheriff? I'd like to call my attorney." Caitlyn stood and gripped the bars of her cell door with her good hand. Her head spun from standing too fast.

Sheriff Tackett sat at his desk and regarded her. "Of course. We'll get to that as soon as I finish my paperwork here."

He seemed pleased to have her behind bars, and Caitlyn knew it was going to be a fight to gain her freedom. She didn't kill Wendy, but trivial facts like that didn't seem to matter to the sheriff. Not as long as he had someone on the hook for the crime—either Dylan or her.

The front door to the office swung open and Colt pushed his way in, laden with a large brown paper bag and two to-go cups. "We didn't finish our coffee this morning, and even prisoners need to be fed." He flashed her a half-smile, but it was less than convincing when no warmth glowed from his expression. The thought that Colt could believe her to be a murderer pierced her heart. How could he possibly think she was capable of killing someone in cold blood?

"Thanks, the coffee smells wonderful." She peered into his eyes, trying to read what was going on in his mind as she reached through the bars for the cup.

He looked away and busied himself with the cinnamon rolls. "I didn't get you anything, Sheriff. I figured you probably already had breakfast."

Sheriff Tackett grunted and opened the filing cabinet. After stuffing a few papers into folders, he stood. "I'll just step out and get my own. Keep a close eye on our prisoner until I come back."

After he went out, Colt pulled a chair over to the bars of the cell. He handed Caitlyn her pastry before sitting down with his own.

"How's Ren?" Caitlyn's heart ached with wanting to see her dog. "Is he going to be okay?"

"I left him with the vet. The doc was getting ready to take x-rays and remove the glass from his paws. He promised to call when he had any information. We'll just have to wait."

"My poor guy. He faced a brutal beating, all for my sake. He didn't deserve that." Caitlyn's voice wavered with emotion, so she took a long swallow of hot coffee to soothe her throat.

"Catie, you swore to me your gun was locked in your truck."

"You can't possibly believe I had anything to do with Wendy's murder. Can you?"

"How do you explain the evidence?"

"The fact that Wendy was killed with a 9mm doesn't mean much. That's a common type of firearm. I've been thinking about it, though. If my gun is the murder weapon, then it makes sense that my fingerprint is on the casing. I'm the one who loaded the magazine. But I didn't kill Wendy! What motive could I possibly have had?" Desperation clawed up Caitlyn's throat.

Colt wrinkled his brow. "They're working on the full ballistics test. But the sheriff is certain your gun is the murder weapon. You told me you had it locked in the safe inside your truck, and that no one knew the combination besides you and your dad. Are you one hundred percent sure no one else knows it? Dylan maybe?"

Caitlyn sighed and propped her chin in her palm. "I'm sure." She raised her gaze to Colt. "Sheriff Tackett found the casing at the scene. I saw him pick it up. But tell me, who discovered the bullet? Was it the CSI or the coroner?"

"It was the CSI. I'll check the chain of custody and find out each step it went through. But what we really need to know is who else could have gained access to your gun."

They finished the rest of their breakfast in silence, both quietly mulling over the case. When they were done eating, Colt collected the trash and stuffed it into the waste bin. He pointed toward the back of the room. "I'll be right back, I'm going to go check the evidence room and see what I can find out." He left through a secured door.

Ten minutes later, Colt rushed back into the office. "Catie, I found something interesting."

She jumped to her feet. "What is it?"

"Sharing this with you could cost me my job, but something is off about the evidence." Hopeful excitement filled his eyes, and he pressed on. "The normal chain of custody for evidence begins with the officers first on scene. Then they turn the scene over to CSI. Any evidence they find is bagged and recorded. It's then taken to the crime lab and signed over to them. Following that, the lab returns the evidence to the investigating law enforcement agency, who locks it up in their own evidence room to await further scrutiny or the trial."

"Right. So, what did you find?" Curiosity edged with an electricity swirled up through Caitlyn's body.

"That's the path that all of our physical evidence in this case took, except for the bullet and its casing." Colt gripped the cell door with one hand and held two clear evidence bags up in the other. "The sheriff found the casing at the scene the day you showed us the body. He bagged it, as he should, and I assume he logged it appropriately. However, that particular bag did not go to the lab until after I confiscated all the firearms from your family's ranch, along with your Glock. I brought all the guns back to the office, and Sheriff Tackett took it from there. He sent all the firearms to the crime lab for the ballistics testing." Colt held up a log form. "It says right here that both this bullet and casing went to the lab with the firearms the same day."

"But you said the crime scene investigator found the slug that killed Wendy and sent it to the lab." Caitlyn gaped at him, her breath suspended in her lungs. "But you're saying they didn't test the bullet until Thursday? How did it get here instead of going to the crime lab?"

"I don't know for sure, but this slug and casing went to the lab together. Maybe he requested these two pieces of evidence go to the lab at the same time? But either way, the sheriff didn't take the firearms to the crime lab until the following day—on Friday. Presumably, the bullet and casing were safe in the evidence locker, here in the office. But it's weird that he didn't send them to the lab immediately." Colt stared at her. The implication of his words bounced in the air.

"Could he possibly have requested the slug from the CSI before she sent her evidence to the lab?" She paced. "I think my attorney can make a compelling argument that there has been a gross mishandling of evidence. It might not prove my innocence, but it sure is enough cause for reasonable doubt." Caitlyn strode the length of the cell and turned. "Speaking of attorneys, I still haven't had a chance to talk to mine."

"What? That's not right. Let me get you the phone." Colt jogged across the room to the sheriff's desk and grabbed the phone. "Do you have his number?"

WHILE CATIE SPOKE to her attorney, Colt returned to the evidence room. He took pictures of each individual evidence bag, including each firearm. He then found the evidence log and snapped a photo of that as well. Something wasn't right, and he intended to find out what it was. By the time he came back into the main office, the sheriff had returned.

"Sheriff, my attorney would like to speak to you." Caitlyn handed her phone through the bars to Tackett, a smug expression sculpting her mouth.

"Sheriff Tackett, here."

Colt kept his own face passive as he watched the Sheriff's coloring go from normal, to red, to puce. By the end of the conversation, the man was pale. He unlocked the jail cell. "You may not have to talk to me until your lawyer gets here, but I believe you're guilty of murder. Don't leave town. I'll be watching you."

Caitlyn didn't waste time responding to him. She hurried to the front of the office. With her good hand, she slung her purse over her shoulder, then asked Colt, "Would you please take me to the vet clinic? I need to see Renegade."

"Of course, come on." Colt accidentally bumped into the sheriff's shoulder as he brushed by and noticed the man wince. "Sorry, sir. Are you okay? I didn't think I hit you that hard."

"I'm fine," the sheriff grumbled. "Old football injury. Must be a storm coming in." Holding his arm, he sat heavily in the chair behind his desk. "As soon as you take Ms. Reed home, get your butt back here. We have a lot to do."

"Let's go." Feeling lighter than he had in hours, Colt opened the door for Caitlyn, and they stepped into the fresh morning air. He still didn't know if Caitlyn was somehow wound up in the murder, but at least he knew there was something else going on behind the scenes and he prayed it would prove her innocence.

"I'm so relieved." Caitlyn clutched onto his sleeve. "With the evidence Sheriff Tackett has, I thought he was going to arrest me for sure. I worried I wouldn't get out of jail since I have no alibi."

"We'll figure it all out, Catie. And though I don't know all that's going on, I promise I'll stand by you, no matter what." He stopped and turned her to face him. It almost hurt to look at her. "I just need you to be completely honest with me. Can you do that?"

Confusion morphed into anger and flashed through Caitlyn's mahogany eyes as she narrowed them. "I'd feel much better if I thought you believed me, *no matter what*. I had absolutely nothing to do with Wendy's murder, nor do I know who did. That is the complete truth." Caitlyn jerked away from him and strode to his Jeep.

Colt got in the driver's seat and closed the door. "I want to believe you, Catie. I'm going to find the murderer, and I agree with you on one thing for sure, something about the evidence and the chain of custody is not right." Colt pulled out onto Main Street and turned toward the veterinarian's office.

The receptionist was at her desk when they entered the clinic. "I'm Caitlyn Reed. The vet has my dog, Renegade, in the back." Caitlyn gripped the counter with her good hand. "Is there any news? How is he doing?" Colt ran his knuckles up and down her shoulder blade, gratified she didn't shake him away. He longed to comfort her, but wasn't sure she'd let him.

"Has the doctor said anything to you?" He prodded the receptionist.

"Doctor Moore hasn't come out of surgery yet. But I'll see what I can find out." The woman went through the swinging door at the back of her cubicle.

Caitlyn turned to him then and buried her face in his chest. He circled his arms around her shoulders and drew her close. His raw heart cracked. How long had he wanted to hold her like this? Wanted her to need him? "Renegade's gonna be okay, Catie. Just think about how much fight he still had left before the animal control officer hit him with the tranquilizer dart." Colt leaned back slightly and tipped her chin up so he could see her eyes. "I sure wouldn't want to be on that dog's bad side."

A smile softened Caitlyn's face. "No chance of that. He has a bro-mance thing going on with you."

"Good to know."

"Yeah, he's a decent judge of character."

"Does that mean there's hope you might forgive me?"

Caitlyn smiled softly at him then. "He's your best ally for that possibility, but I think the bigger question is, do you believe me?" The receptionist returned to her desk, followed by the veterinarian, saving him from having to answer.

"Hello, Caitlyn. How are you feeling? The deputy tells me someone attacked you?" His concerned eyes peered at her bruised face through his trifocals.

Caitlyn half lifted her sling. "I'll be all right. Just a few bumps, that's all. How is Renegade?"

"I'm happy to report I was able to remove all the glass from Renegade's paws. However, he's in greater danger from the head injuries he sustained. Obviously, unlike humans, I cannot ask him questions about how he feels. So, I'm going to assume the worst. I'd like him to stay here at the clinic where I can keep him mildly sedated and enforce rest. Belgians are high energy dogs, and I doubt he would take it easy at home. There is a minor fracture in his skull, but I have every reason to believe it will heal well. We need to keep any swelling down. Which, of course, is another reason I'd like him to stay here."

Caitlyn's voice cracked. "I understand. Can I see him?"

"Yes, of course. I'll take you back. He's sleeping but, who

knows? He may be able to hear your voice, and I'm sure that would comfort him."

"Thank you, Doctor." Caitlyn slipped her hand into Colt's, winding her fingers around his. He gripped them and followed her to see her dog, knowing in that moment that he would follow her anywhere, even if it meant he'd be visiting her through a plexiglass barrier in prison.

The vet had scrubbed Renegade's blood-matted fur clean, and there were three shaved bald spots on his head where stitches held his wounds closed. A small cry escaped Caitlyn's throat when she saw him, and Colt pulled her close.

"Remember, the doc says he's going to be okay."

"He suffered all of this because of me." Caitlyn searched Colt's face.

He cupped her cheek and brushed her forehead with his lips, murmuring against her skin. "Because he loves you."

Caitlyn hugged him tight then, causing hope and despair to swirl like oil and water in his gut. Finally, she seemed to open herself up to him. And he loved her, whatever her part in Wendy's murder might have been.

They didn't stay long, knowing Renegade needed his rest. It had been an exhausting morning, and they agreed they could both use another dose of caffeine. "Besides," Caitlyn said. "I need to check the schedule to see when my next shift is."

Together, they walked up the road to the café. Coming out the door as they stepped in was Jim Hague. He stopped when he saw them. "I thought you were supposed to be in jail," he snarled at Caitlyn.

"Obviously, there wasn't enough evidence to hold me there." Caitlyn squared her shoulders and reached out to clutch his arm. "I promise, I had nothing to do with Wendy's death."

He jerked away from her. "Then it was your brother. One

of you, or both, took my Wendy from me." He glared at Caitlyn as he made his way past them—his slate eyes cold.

Caitlyn watched him go. "Does it seem to you like he's limping?" she asked as Jim hobbled down the steps.

Colt turned to look. "A little, I guess." They stood side-by-side and studied the man as he ambled down the walk.

"How did Jim and Wendy know each other? He's not from around here, is he?"

"No. He has been working construction at the new golf course for the past year or so. I think he's originally from Nebraska."

_____

23

Caitlyn and Colt took their coffees to go and walked together back down the street to his Jeep. The sun was high and hot, so Caitlyn shrugged out of her sweatshirt and asked Colt to help her tie the arms around her waist. She was uncomfortable leaving her cabin wide open to anyone who might come by and was anxious to get home. A broken living room window was an invitation for wildlife or transients to enter. Not that they had many of the latter in their rural county. She didn't believe for one minute the intruder who broke in last night was a random burglar. None of her things had seemed out of place that morning, and she was fairly sure the man hadn't stolen anything, but she still needed to sort through her home and check.

Colt rolled down the windows of his Jeep as they drove through town. "I can help you clean up the broken glass at your house before I return to work, if you want."

Caitlyn smiled at him. "The sheriff was pretty clear. You better get right back to the office. I can handle it." In all honesty, she was nervous about being at the cabin alone without Renegade. But she wasn't about to admit that to

Colt, and besides, she'd have to face the damage sometime. Caitlyn reclined against the car seat and sipped her coffee. Breathing in the fresh mountain air, she wondered if last night's intruder had anything to do with the murder investigation. Her mind rolled across the evidence as she gazed out the window.

"Stop!"

Colt slammed on the brakes. Coffee splashed down the front of his shirt. "What the—?" he grumbled as he wiped at the wet fabric.

Caitlyn grimaced. "Sorry about that." She pointed to what had caused her to shout. "Pull over."

"What's the matter?" Colt asked as he parked his Jeep on the side of the street.

Caitlyn flung her door open and jumped out. Colt was quick to follow.

"What's going on, Catie?"

"This car." She ran to the front of an older model Toyota parked at the curb. "Look here. The corner of this vehicle is smashed—the turn light is broken."

Colt came up behind her and peered over her shoulder. "So? What about it?"

Caitlyn crouched down and studied the dent in the car. "Silver paint." She took out her phone and snapped several pictures.

Colt stepped back and crossed his arms over his chest. "What are you talking about? Whose car is this?"

"This is the car that hit me. See the silver paint? That's from my truck!"

"Hit you? When?"

Caitlyn thought back to the near miss she'd had the evening she left her parents' house after dinner. Then she gasped. "That was the same night as Wendy's murder!" Caitlyn stood, covering her mouth with her hand as she mentally sifted through the course of events. She stared up at Colt. "The same night someone almost drove me off the road into the river, after I left my parents' house."

"Someone hit you?" Colt was obviously having trouble making sense of her story.

"Yes. I had just turned onto the forest highway, when out of nowhere headlights were coming at me broadside. I slammed on my brakes, and the car swerved, but it still clipped my front end. I thought I was going to slip over the edge. My tires skidded terribly close, but fortunately they caught hold at the last minute."

Shock registered on Colt's face. "Why didn't you call the sheriff's office?"

"Because, I didn't have a description of the car. All I could see were the taillights. The only thing I knew was it was a compact. I figured it was just some kids who'd been up the forest access road drinking and hooking up."

"You still should've called it in. That's a hit-and-run accident. Plus, they damaged your truck. Your insurance might not pay for it without an incident report."

Caitlyn looked up at the house the car sat in front of. "I know you're right, but I had other things on my mind. I had just had a big fight with Dylan, and all I wanted was to get home." She jutted her chin toward the residence. "Isn't this where Eleanor Smooter lives?"

Colt followed her gaze. "I think so. Why?"

"Because, someone parked this car in front of her house. But it's not her car, I don't think. Let's go ask." Caitlyn marched up the walk and climbed the porch steps to the front door.

"Wait, for me." Colt rushed after her.

Caitlyn pushed the doorbell twice. She waited half a breath before she knocked angrily on the thick wood. It took a minute or so before they heard footsteps and the heavy door swung open.

"Caitlyn. Deputy Branson, how nice to see the two of you." Eleanor Smooter pulled her cardigan together at her neck and glowered at them, blinking through her cat eye glasses and pasting a plastic smile on her face.

Irritation flared between Caitlyn's temples, causing her bruised brain to throb. "Whose—"

Colt put his hand on Caitlyn's shoulder to calm her. "Good morning, Ms. Smooter. How are you today?" Colt offered her his extra engaging grin. One that had caused Caitlyn to swoon more than once in her life.

The woman, somewhat mollified by his manners, returned his smile with a slight softening of her own. "Well, it's a little early to receive visitors."

"We apologize for that, ma'am. But we're wondering if you might be able to help us?"

Eleanor patted her black coif before answering Colt. "I can't imagine how?"

Caitlyn swallowed her desire to shake the woman and force her to answer. Fortunately, Colt handled the situation.

He gestured to the curb. "Do you happen to know who the owner of that vehicle parked in front of your house, is?"

"Why do you ask, Deputy?"

"Please, Ms. Smooter, do you know who parked that car there?"

Eleanor chewed on her answer before she gave it. "That car belongs to my houseguest."

Caitlyn looked past Eleanor into her house, but saw no one else there. "Do you mean the woman who was with you when I saw you at the Mercantile last week? Maribel Martin, I think her name was?"

"Yes, that's her."

Caitlyn couldn't reconcile why a pregnant woman would

come careening out of a mountain access road at eleven o'clock at night. "How long has she been in town?"

Eleanor crossed her arms, and with one hand fingered the loose skin drooping from her turkey-like neck. "Why do you ask? Is there a problem?"

Colt leaned in with his charm. "No problem at all, Ms. Smooter. We just noticed her front indicator is broken. I'd hate for her to get a ticket if she were driving through town with her turn light in that state." He gave her a crooked grin that made him look like an adorable, but mischievous boy. It occurred to Caitlyn that she'd have to be on the lookout for that deceptive charm herself. "Do you know if anyone else has driven her car while she's been here?"

Eleanor frowned and narrowed her eyes. "I don't believe so. I'll tell her about the light. Thank you for stopping by." She edged the door shut.

Colt lifted a hand in farewell. "Have a nice day." He took Caitlyn's arm and turned her from the door as it closed behind them.

"What are you doing?" Caitlyn pulled away from him. "I wanted to talk to Maribel—ask her if she hit me."

"And do you think you would've gotten an honest answer?" Colt walked Caitlyn back to his Jeep. Once inside, he said, "All I can do is keep an eye on the car. If you would have filed a report, we could have impounded the vehicle and tested to see if the paint matched your truck."

"This is so frustrating." Caitlyn clicked on her seatbelt. "I wonder if all the things that have happened recently are connected somehow, but I can't seem to make them come together."

"It is strange. Are you thinking there's a link between the car and the murder?" Colt drove them out of town toward Caitlyn's ranch.

"I'm not sure, but I'd like to go check out that forest access road."

"Not today. You're going home to rest. You have a concussion, remember?"

"Let's try to connect the dots."

Colt studied her for a moment before he returned his focus to driving. "How do you mean?"

"Well, a compact car hits my truck and nearly sends me over the edge of the road to the river below. There's a murder. The sheriff accuses my brother. You confiscate all our firearms. Last night, someone attacked me in my home. Then, it looks like *my* gun might be the murder weapon. It seems like a lot to happen all in one week." She tapped her fingers on the open window casing.

"The accident could've been a coincidence. But the fact that a man broke into your house and attacked you is a whole different matter. I want to know why. Was it the murderer? Could it have been Dylan? What did the attacker hope to gain?"

Caitlyn spun in her seat, spikes of anger shooting like arrows behind her eyes. "Dylan would never attack me. I can't believe you would even think that."

"We have to consider everything, Catie. I agree, Dylan wouldn't want to hurt you... normally. But he's been angry with you for a long time, and if he killed Wendy, his back could be against the wall. Does he know you've been investigating this case on your own?"

"No!" Her answer flew out of her mouth, but she paused to think about the possibility. "I don't think so." Caitlyn fidgeted in her seat and pressed her palm down the length of her thigh. "Actually, I did mention to my dad and Dylan that I was going to look into the case." *Damn it.*

Colt glanced at her before returning his gaze to the road. "So, if Dylan came to see you and happened to notice your wall of evidence... with his name on the suspect list... That could have thrown him over the edge. Don't you think?"

"Not that far over the edge." She hoped.

"Today, you told me that Renegade was an excellent judge of character."

"Yeah?"

"From what I've seen, Renegade doesn't like Dylan. Why is that?"

"It's not that he doesn't like him, he just doesn't appreciate it when Dylan is angry with me." A soft laugh crossed her lips. "Ren's extremely protective."

"That's obvious." Colt reached for her hand. "Catie, are you sure you're telling me everything?"

"What are you getting at?"

"If Dylan murdered Wendy, you can't save him." He took a deep breath and let it all out at once. "If you're an accomplice, tell me now, and I'll help you the best I can."

Caitlyn stared at him. She pulled her hand back, and her jaw dropped open, finding no words. Even if she had some, the aching stone lodged in her throat would never let them pass. *He actually thinks I could be involved in a murder.* "Colt, I had nothing to do with Wendy's murder. How many times do I have to tell you that? I can't believe you don't trust me."

Colt kept his gaze straight out the windshield, the muscles in his jaw bunched into a corded knot.

COLT WANTED, with everything that he was, to believe Caitlyn, but evidence that she knew more than she admitted was lining up against her. If she truly had nothing to do with the murder, why would someone try to run her off the road? What about the note she found? Was the attack at her cabin a warning to keep her quiet? There were too many unanswered questions. Colt dropped Caitlyn off at home, and since she insisted she could handle the cleanup herself, he focused on investigating the break-in.

"Before you sweep, let me gather the glass with the blood on it to send to the lab." After collecting the samples he needed, Colt examined both the front and back doors, but didn't find any signs of forced entry. Next, he checked each of the windows, but there wasn't so much as a scrape or bent screen. "Do you lock your doors when you leave?"

"Not usually." Caitlyn grimaced and shrugged.

That wasn't surprising. Most people in the country left their doors open. "Well, from now on, you need to. Okay?"

"Yeah. It's just that with Ren, I never figured I had to."

Colt responded with an arched eyebrow.

"I will." She rolled her eyes, but inwardly she knew she'd never leave a door unlocked again.

"Good." Colt dusted the doors and frames for finger-prints. There were many, making it impossible to prove much. "Do you want help boarding up your window?"

"No. I'll get it. If I can't find a big enough board in the garage, I may need to go to the hardware store."

"Okay. I'm gonna head out to your family's ranch after lunch, then. I have a few more questions for Dylan." He left the cabin and turned back to wave when he reached his car.

Caitlyn leaned against the front doorjamb with her arms crossed. "I didn't do it, you know."

He gave her a curt nod and tried to smile, but his features were stiff. *I just hope you're telling me all you know.*

Colt drove back through town and checked in at the Sheriff's Office. After lunch, he headed west to the Reed's family ranch. On his way, Colt decided to have a look at the forest access road Caitlyn told him about. He slowed down as he neared the turnoff to the ranch. Even so, he almost missed the overgrown road. "Road" was a generous term for a six-foot-wide grass and rock two-track pathway that the forest service cut through the trees probably fifty years ago, or more. A wheeled vehicle had recently matted down the tall grasses, but unless he was searching for them, he wouldn't have seen the tracks.

Colt switched to four-wheel drive when he turned on the path. He followed the trail as it veered upward, bouncing through aspen groves, high meadows, and thick patches of pine. Spring wild flowers were in bloom. He tucked this secret location away in his mind. *This would make the perfect place for a long private picnic.* He pictured Catie sitting on a blanket with her face tilted up to the sun.

At the top of the ridge, the path veered to the right and opened up to a flat rocky area. Colt parked his car. The air was crisp, prickling his nose with the sharp scent of pine. He breathed deep and, scanning the surrounding mountains, attempted to reconnoiter his location. Behind a row of trees stood a barbed wire fence, which he followed until he came to a gate. The back of his neck prickled. He hadn't realized that the rarely used road lead up to the BLM side of the gate on top of the ridge where Catie found the body.

Adrenaline surged through his brain, and his pulse flew. Caitlyn was right to want to investigate the forest access road. Careful of where he stepped, Colt studied the ground around the gate, walking methodically back to his Jeep. He stopped cold. *Tire tracks!*

In the silty dirt about twenty feet from the gate, Colt recognized the unmistakable imprint of a tire tread preserved in dried mud. Skirting the area, he ran back to his car to gather both his casting and fingerprint kits. The new impression evidence sent his nerves jumping, and he dropped his keys when he tried to open the back end of the Jeep.

After photographing the tire tracks, Colt mixed water

and some dry dental-stone material making a thick, smooth consistency. He poured it into the furrows of the tread prints, then left that to dry while he went to brush the gates for fingerprints. Of course, that was a crap shoot. Hundreds of people probably left prints on the metal gate over the years, including Caitlyn and Dylan.

What he found, however, was more interesting than he expected. There were no prints at all. Someone had wiped the gate clean. That made the tire tracks all that more meaningful, and Colt was thankful there had been no rain since the murder.

After the casting dried, Colt carefully peeled the impressions up and placed them in a protective box. He searched the area once more for any evidence he might have missed. Finding nothing, he drove back down the mountain to the highway. The road was steep at the bottom, and Colt imagined a car flying out of the trees and swerving to miss a truck on the road. His chest tightened and air pressed out of his lung as his gut cinched tight. He closed his eyes against the mental image of Caitlyn's truck tumbling down the cliff, crashing into the river far below.

He shook the thought from his mind and turned right onto the highway. It was time to check on Dylan. When he got to the ranch, he found Dylan stacking hay in the loafing shed behind the barn. Colt pulled a pair of leather gloves from the console of his car. He figured Dylan might be more willing to talk if he had some help with his work.

In silence, the men stacked six bales of hay before Dylan asked, "How can I help you, Deputy? I can't imagine you just meandered out here to help me stack hay."

"You're right. I have a few questions, but I don't mind giving you a hand while I ask them." Colt tossed a bale up to Dylan and noticed that he only used one arm to snug it up.

"What's on your mind?"

"I'm wondering where you were last night?"

"Don't tell me there was another murder?" Dylan glowered down at him.

"No, nothing like that." *Luckily. Though whoever attacked Caitlyn probably would have killed her if Renegade didn't chase him off.* "Just wondering if you were out?" Colt kept his tone casual as he tossed up another bale.

Again, Dylan lifted it and tightened the stack using only his left hand.

"My attorney told me not to answer any questions without him present."

Colt held his hand up to shade his eyes as he looked up at Dylan. "Are you okay? Seems like you're favoring your arm."

"Nope. I'm fine."

"Can I take a look?"

"What? At my arm?" Dylan scoffed. "You got a warrant?"

"I'm just concerned." He wouldn't get anywhere by pissing the man off.

Dylan glanced down at his right arm and then leveled his gaze at Colt and shrugged. "I got yanked off my horse this morning when I was roping a cow. Landed on it wrong. It's just sore."

"You sure it isn't broken?"

Dylan cocked his head as he looked down at Colt. "When did you become Nurse Nightingale? I told you it was fine. Just a little sore that's all."

"Have you talked to Catie lately?"

"What's this all about, Deputy?"

Colt perched his hands on his hips and thought about how much information he wanted to give to Dylan. The thing was, Caitlyn was his sister. If he wasn't the one who attacked her, he should at least know it happened. "Somebody broke into Caitlyn's cabin last night—"

Dylan jumped off the haystack. "What? Who? Is she okay?"

"The intruder attacked her, she has a concussion." Colt watched Dylan closely. "But other than that, she's going to be all right."

"How did the guy get past her dog?"

Colt looked pointedly at Dylan's arm. "He didn't."

24

Caitlyn swept up the glass pieces shattered across her living room floor. Her heart wrenched when she saw her dog's blood smeared on some of the sharp edges. Frustrated by one armed sweeping, she yanked off the sling holding her injured limb. After she cleaned up the best she could, she vacuumed, turning the machine off several times to listen for sounds she thought she'd heard. She wiped the floor over again with wet paper towels. Satisfied she'd cleaned up all the splintered shards, she went to search her belongings.

Parts of the murder board on her dining room wall were torn down. It was weird she hadn't noticed that this morning. Wondering if the intruder had stolen anything she hadn't realized, Caitlyn entered her bedroom. She shuddered at the thought of an unknown man in her space, touching her things. Had his fingers run over her intimate items? She glanced over her shoulder before she opened the top drawer of her dresser.

Under the few pieces of lingerie she owned, she reached for a velvet box. Opening it, she was relieved to see her grandmother's pearls still nestled safely in their place. Besides her firearms, that necklace was the only thing of value she owned. With sorrow laden nostalgia, Caitlyn smoothed her fingertips over the cold, smooth surface of the pearls and thought of the woman she missed so deeply. Her eyes watered and her nose ran, her exhaustion keeping her emotions on the surface.

She went into the bathroom for a tissue and clicked on the light. In front of her reflection in the mirror above the sink, written in red marker, were the words, "Stay out of it! Or Else!" Chills coursed through her body and she dropped her gaze to the sink—and screamed.

Wadded up inside the sink was the dead body of a squirrel. Someone had broken its neck. Caitlin ran out and huddled in the corner of her bedroom. Fighting tears and forcing herself to slow her breathing, she thought of what to do. That bastard had come back while she was gone.

Tires scrabbled over the gravel outside. A searing chill spurred up Caitlyn's spine, spiking alarm bells inside her sore head. Her heart careened spastically against her ribs and she ran to her walk-in closet. At the back, she thrust her winter jackets to the side, and reached for a rifle that had been in her family since before it was necessary to register firearms. No one except her father knew she had it, and she hadn't bothered to tell Colt when he was confiscating all their firearms. She kept it loaded, so when she grabbed it, all she needed to do was seat a round in the chamber. Of course, that was a challenge one handed.

Feeling more confident than she had mere seconds before, Caitlyn tip-toed out of her closet, through her room, and peered out her bedroom door. Listening hard, she heard no movement. Caitlyn stepped quietly out her door and crept down the hall, keeping her back to the wall until she got to the living room. Still, she saw no one, but the entrance door remained unlocked and the picture window was open to the breeze.

Caitlyn darted to the front wall and edged her way to the side of the open living room window. She leveled her rifle and swung it around through the opening in the wall, sucking in a breath as the muzzle pointed directly into the chest of a large man standing on her porch.

"What the hell?" the man growled

Caitlyn stepped back, but kept the gun pointed at him. "What are you doing creeping around my cabin?"

Her brother batted the rifle barrel away. "Get that out of my face. You know better than to aim a gun at someone unless you intend to shoot them."

"I did intend to shoot." Caitlyn lowered the muzzle. "What are you doing here, Dylan?"

"Your boyfriend paid me a visit this afternoon. He told me someone broke into your house last night and attacked you." His voice softened. "Are you okay?" Dylan surveyed the empty window frame before he scanned his sister up and down.

"He's not my boyfriend."

"Have you told him that?"

"What do you want, Dylan?"

"I came to check on you. Colt said you had a concussion." He reached for her and touched her cheek. "Your face is bruised. When I find the asshole who hit you, I'm going to kill him."

"Not words you should fling around carelessly, these days." Caitlyn tossed him a wry expression and rested the rifle against the wall. She went to open the front door. "Come on in. I'm fine, but the bastard put my dog in the hospital."

"That's what I heard. Did he steal anything?" Dylan came

through the door and removed his hat. "What do you think he wanted?"

"That's the million-dollar question, because nothing is missing. Want a beer?"

"Sure, but let's get your front window boarded up first. Do you have some plywood?"

While they rummaged in the garage to find what they needed to seal up the window temporarily, Caitlyn told her brother what she found in the bathroom.

"You need to report this before we clean it up."

She nodded and went to the kitchen. She pulled two bottles of beer from her fridge and handed one to her brother. "Thanks for your help."

"Sure." Dylan walked across the living room and took in Caitlyn's makeshift evidence wall. "What's all this about?" He sipped his brew and scanned the information she'd tacked up.

"Guess whoever left the squirrel didn't like my collage." Caitlyn picked up several papers that had been torn from the wall, tacked them back up and reattached the red string. "Like I told you and Dad, I don't trust the sheriff to do a complete investigation, so I'm doing one of my own. I guess, I'm trying to keep you out of prison." Caitlyn gulped half of her beer down. "You didn't kill Wendy, did you?"

Dylan faced her and took a minute before he answered. "Even though you have my name listed as a suspect, you know I didn't."

"I don't *believe* you did, but where were you during those unaccounted-for hours the night Wendy was killed?" Caitlyn stood next to Dylan, and they both studied the murder wall. "Did you drive down to Sundance to see her?" Dylan tilted his head and looked at her. "Sundance?"

Caitlyn released some of the tension she held in her bunched shoulders. "You didn't know she was there?"

"The last time I saw Wendy was at the Tipsy Cow. I swear that's true."

"I believe you Dylan, but why won't you tell anyone where you were after that?"

Again he was silent for a long moment. "I'll tell you, Caitlyn, but you can't share this information with anyone. Not even with Colt."

"Why?"

Dylan walked to the front window and stood with his back to her. He stared out across her front yard. "When I left the Tipsy Cow, I ran into Heather Mansfield in the parking lot. You remember her from school, don't you?" Caitlyn nodded. "Well, anyway, she was just getting there. She was upset, and frankly, so was I, so we decided to go have a drink together by ourselves to commiserate—I was with her."

"Okay, that's terrific news. Then Heather can give you an alibi. You're off the hook!"

Dylan swung around to face her, his expression serious. "No. I mean... I was *with* her."

Slowly it dawned on Caitlyn what her brother was saying. "But Dylan—she's married."

"Separated."

"You're splitting hairs."

"I know. It was wrong. We'd both had too much to drink. We were feeling sorry for ourselves, and it just happened. The thing is, she wants to get back together with her husband. She loves him. So, I don't want to drag her through the mud and ruin her chances."

"For God's sake, Dylan. This is your life we're talking about. You've got to stop getting drunk and sleeping around. It doesn't solve your problems." Caitlyn was incredulous. "You could go to prison."

"Well, it hasn't gone that far yet. I didn't kill Wendy—but

somebody did. If the sheriff finds out who it was, I'll be off the hook without wrecking things for Heather."

"Dylan, the sheriff doesn't care who actually killed Wendy. He just wants someone to blame, so he can look good for solving a crime. You can't put your life in hands like that."

Her brother shifted his gaze to the wall behind her. "You're probably right. But I can trust you. Looks like you're investigating the murder." A soft smile peeked out from his dark beard. "God must have cut you from the same cloth as Logan. Our brother would be proud of you."

A rush of emotion flooded through Caitlyn and clogged her throat. This was the most Dylan had said to her in almost nine months, and possibly the kindest words ever. Tears pricked the back of her eyes and she wanted to throw her arms around him. But Dylan wasn't a demonstrative man. He was not the kind of guy who appreciated hugging, so she stayed where she was.

"Okay, Dyl. I'll keep your secret unless it comes to a point when we need to disclose the information in order to save your life. Deal?"

Dylan looked her in the eye. "Let's try not to let it get that far."

Caitlyn nodded and pivoted so she stood next to him, both of them facing the murder wall. "I really appreciate you coming out here to check on me, Dylan. It means a lot." Caitlyn leaned to her right and bumped his shoulder with hers.

"Just because I'm mad at you, doesn't mean I don't care about you." They stood, not looking at each other while they spoke.

"Can we talk about why you're angry with me?"

Dylan sighed from the depths of his being. He crossed his arms over his chest, then grunted and shook out his right hand "I'd rather not. It's irreconcilable. There's no fixing it and thinking about it just pisses me off all over again."

"But can't you understand, even a little, that I want to be out on my own?" Caitlyn pulled a chair from the dining table and sat. She spun her beer bottle around in wobbly circles, waiting for her brother to answer.

"That's the only part I *do* understand." Dylan also took a chair and angled himself to face her. "But why didn't you talk to *me* about it? Instead, you went straight to Dad."

"Dad is who I should have gone to. Don't you think? His name is the one on the deed." She took a swig of beer. "Either way, I didn't mean to hurt your feelings."

Dylan worked his jaw and picked at the paper label on his bottle. "This isn't about hurting my feelings, Caitlyn. Dad's name *is* on the deed, but that doesn't mean he's on top of the day-to-day running of the ranch."

Caitlyn's stomach balled up with concern. "What are you getting at?"

"Reed Ranch has been struggling financially for several years. We needed two or three years in a row of high cattle prices at the market to make up for it."

"I gathered that, and I know Dad pulling my share of the ranch out in cash, made things tight. I'm sorry about that. It's why instead of getting a job, I've been trying to work at the ranch. That way you don't have to hire anyone."

Dylan leveled his gaze at her for an uncomfortable moment. "It's a lot worse than not being able to hire a ranch hand, Caitlyn."

"How bad is it?"

He released another gust of air. "As you know, cattle prices have continued to drop this year. At this point, I can't afford to buy enough grain to get the cows through 'til market next fall." Dylan scratched his chin under his beard and dropped his voice. "And, I'm not gonna be able to make the mortgage payment next month." Their eyes met, searching for each other's reaction in the silence.

"I had no idea. Why didn't you say something before Dad went to the bank?"

"I didn't want him to know how bad it was. I thought I could regain the gap your inheritance caused by the end of the year. We had high hopes for the cattle sale last fall." He rubbed his face with his hands and mumbled through them. "It really sucks that I'm going to be the one who loses the family ranch."

Caitlyn reached for his arm. "No, Dylan. It isn't you... it's me. It's my fault." Caitlyn stood and walked around the room. Her thoughts crashing against the sickness swimming in her belly. Her rash decision—her longing for independence—had put her entire family's future at risk. How could she have been so stupid? So selfish? She spun to face her brother. "We can fix this, I know we can. I'll put this place on the market. I'll move back home and work for free."

"I appreciate that, Caitlyn. But there's not time. Even if you found someone to buy your place tomorrow, which you wouldn't, you'd still have to go through the closing process. The mortgage is due next week."

"Have you talked to the bank? Maybe we can make a partial payment?"

"Yes, they're willing to work with us, but that's only going to buy us a couple months."

"Have you talked to Logan?"

"He's already disappointed in me enough."

"He's not disappointed. He's just worried about you, that's all." Caitlyn tossed her chin in the air and stared hard at the ceiling. "I need to get a proper job." But what could she do that would make enough money to pay the mortgage on her family's ranch? There wasn't a lot of work around here. "Maybe, I could find something in Gillette, or Sheridan?"

"Maybe." Dylan looked past her, over her shoulder, at the murder wall. "What kind of work would you look for?"

"I don't know." The familiar emptiness spurred by her lack of direction weighed heavily upon her chest and shoulders.

Dylan leaned closer to the wall, reading some of the finer print Caitlyn had scratched in her notes. "What about law enforcement? Your degree is in criminal justice, and it seems like you're doing a better job than the sheriff on Wendy's murder case." He turned around and pierced Caitlyn with dark brown eyes that matched hers.

Caitlyn's gaze shifted from her brother to the wall behind him and back. "I don't know about better…"

"It looks to me like you're letting the evidence tell its own story, rather than jumping to conclusions. That's more than the sheriff is doing."

"He just wants a conviction. I think he sees being the sheriff as a political position instead of a law enforcement career."

"Already you sound better than him."

"Well, Colt has been a big help…"

Dylan offered her a rare grin. "You ever going to give that boy a chance?"

Hot self-consciousness bloomed in her cheeks. "I don't know. There's a lot of history there."

"Yeah, everyone has history, Caitlyn. No one is perfect. But Colt has been pining after you since high school." He chuckled. "He's a good guy. Put the man out of his misery."

Caitlyn's lips curled, and she bit down on the smile. "Maybe. He's been pretty great during all of this." She tossed her empty beer bottle into the trashcan and spoke over her shoulder. "But I don't know how I feel about him thinking I could have had something to do with Wendy's murder."

"Wait—he thinks what?"

25

The following morning, Caitlyn drove into town. She hadn't heard from Dr. Moore yet, but it was still early. She couldn't wait to see Renegade. When she paused at the first stop sign on Main Street, she noticed Dylan's truck parked in front of the feed store. Her brother came out through the double doors followed by Jim, the owner of the shop. Dylan pushed his hands into his pockets and said a few words to him, then Jim gripped Dylan's shoulder. By the look of things, her brother was probably asking to extend his credit.

Caitlyn choked on the wad of guilt that knotted itself inside her throat, knowing how hard it was for her brother to ask for help. She clicked on her signal and turned into the parking lot as the men shook hands and Jim returned to the store. Caitlyn parked next to Dylan's rig and got out.

"Hey, Dyl. I didn't expect to see you in town this morning." Caitlyn rounded his truck and met him at the driver's side door.

"Just asking for a little more time to make my credit payment. Jim agreed to give me a couple months. He's a great guy." Dylan's color was high, and Caitlyn knew that his loss of pride cost him far more than a higher interest rate.

"I'm so sorry, Dylan. I have a charge card that Dad opened for me before I went to college. The credit limit isn't very high, but it's something."

"Thanks Caitlyn, I'll let you know if I need to take you up on that." He shoved his hands into his jeans pockets. "What are you doing in town?"

"I came in to see Renegade. I'm hoping to take him home this morning."

"Want me to go to the vet with you?"

"Sure." Caitlyn's chest flooded with love. It'd been a long time since she and Dylan had acted like siblings. Maybe he cared more than she thought? "If you'd like, we can leave your truck here and take mine."

"That works. Jim has some bags of grain he still needs to load in the bed of my truck, anyway."

They got into Caitlyn's F-150 and drove to the veterinary clinic. The doctor arrived several minutes after they did. Caitlyn waved at him as she stepped out.

"Good morning, Caitlyn." He shook Dylan's hand. "I suppose you're here to see Renegade?"

"Sure am. I'm hoping he's ready to go home?" She and Dylan followed the vet into the building.

"I'm undecided about releasing him today. I did an MRI yesterday, and I think there may still be some bleeding inside your pup's skull. I'll look again this morning, but if it hasn't stopped, I can't let you take him home. Not yet."

Caitlyn's legs quit working. She stood stock still, frozen by the doctor's words. Dylan rested a hand on her shoulder. "What does that mean, Doc? He's going to be okay, isn't he?"

The vet slid into his lab coat before he faced them. "I hope so. But it's too soon to tell. Are you planning to be in town for a little while? I can run my tests right away and let you know."

"I'll wait here, in the waiting room." Caitlyn swallowed what felt like gravel in her throat. "Can I see him?"

Dr. Moore nodded and gestured for them to follow. He led them to the stainless-steel kennel that held her dog. When Renegade saw her, he jumped to his bandaged feet. The cone attached to his collar jammed against the top of the enclosure, and his tail swept heartily back and forth. "He sure is glad to see you," Dylan encouraged.

"Hey, buddy." Caitlyn's voice swam in her unshed tears as she raced to kneel in front of the kennel. "*Lehne*," she told him. "You need to stay off your feet!" Renegade laid down, but his tail continued to beat the sides and floor of the kennel.

Caitlyn peered up at the vet. "Other than his bandaged paws, he looks fine."

The man looked down at her with a kind smile. "And we can certainly hope that he is, but I want to be sure."

"I know." Caitlyn stuck her fingers through the metal mesh door, and Renegade licked them. Dylan crouched behind her. "My money's on Ren. He's the scrappiest dog I've ever known."

It surprised Caitlyn that Renegade didn't growl at Dylan, as close as he was. It seemed to her, over the last month, her dog would have preferred to chase her brother up to South Dakota. But today, he acted pleased to see him. She considered that a good sign. Maybe he sensed the change in mood between Dylan and her.

"Okay, why don't you two let me get to work?" The veterinarian started adjusting dials on one of his machines.

"I'll just be in the other room, boy. Hopefully, we can both go home together this afternoon." Renegade answered her with a hopeful yip. Caitlyn blinked up at her brother. "He doesn't understand why I'm leaving him here."

Dylan put his arm around her shoulder and led her to the waiting area. "No, but he trusts you."

Caitlyn nodded and glanced back at her dog as the door swung closed. She sat down in the waiting room. "You don't have to wait here with me. I know you have work to do."

"Are you sure?" Dylan stood looking down at her.

Part of her didn't want to let her brother go. It was so good to have him talking to her again without anger in his voice, but she'd already caused enough trouble. "I'll be okay, and I'll keep you posted."

He gave her a nod. "Good. I'll talk to you later, then." Dylan left to walk the few blocks back to the feed store.

Caitlyn had been waiting about a half hour when she called Colt. His phone rang twice before he answered. "Hey, I was just about to call you."

"Hi. Thought I'd let you know I'm over at the vet's."

"Are you picking up Renegade?"

"No, not yet. The doctor thinks he might still have some bleeding in his brain." Caitlyn closed her eyes against the thought.

"I'm sorry to hear that, Catie." The timbre in his voice soothed her.

"Dr. Moore is running another MRI. He should know something more definite soon."

"Well, it's good that Renegade has a safe place to be."

Caitlyn gripped her phone at the change in his tone. "What do you mean?"

Colt paused. "The full ballistics report came back on your gun."

"And?"

"And, the Sheriff has ordered me to arrest you."

Her heart jolted with an electric bolt. "He what? On what grounds?"

"Stay there, I'll be right over." Colt ended the call.

Caitlyn peered at the dark screen of her phone for a second. She didn't need this—not right now. She opened her purse and practically threw her cell inside. The last thing she wanted was to have to deal with the sheriff's poor investigative skills today. Not while Renegade was going through his tests and the extent of the damage was uncertain.

Several minutes later, Colt walked through the door into the clinic. "Any news on Ren?"

Caitlyn shook her head, staring hard at him to keep the unwanted tears out of her eyes. "What's going on with the sheriff now? He told you to arrest me? I can't believe him."

"The thing is, Catie. He has enough solid evidence to hold you this time."

"That's impossible. There can't be evidence of me perpetrating a crime I didn't commit." Red anger splashed like waves behind her eyes and she flew to her feet.

"The ballistics test proves the 9mm slug that killed Wendy definitely came from your Glock." Colt regarded her with an expression she couldn't read.

"I don't see how that's possible. But even if it is, that doesn't mean *I* murdered her. I didn't." Something shuttered inside Colt's eyes. "Colt?"

"I'm sure we'll get to the bottom of it. But for now, Caitlyn, you are under arrest for the murder of Wendy Gessler. You have the right to remain silent..." He quoted her Miranda rights. Caitlyn's jaw fell open and her stomach dropped. She couldn't believe that Colt would arrest her.

Colt took her by her unhurt arm. "I don't have to cuff you, do I?"

"You wouldn't dare." She glared at him, putting on a tough exterior while inside she fell apart.

"I sure don't want to." He dropped his gaze and refused to meet hers.

"Colt. You can't possibly think…" Her stomach curdled.

"I'm just following orders… and looking at the evidence." He escorted her outside and opened the back door of his Jeep for her.

"Seriously?"

"Please get in."

Caitlyn sat in the back seat of the Jeep—where criminals rode. Her mind reeled at the fact that Colt wasn't one hundred percent certain about her innocence. He actually thought she could be a murderer. *I was right about him all along. I can't trust him. He knows nothing about loyalty.* "I'm calling my lawyer." Caitlyn reached inside her purse and snatched out her cell phone, punching at numbers on the screen. She spoke to her attorney, filling him in on all the details she knew so far. "I won't. Okay. I'll see you this afternoon."

Colt parked behind the Sheriff's office and escorted her inside through the back door, but Caitlyn didn't care about her privacy. She was too mad.

"I told you to let me handle it!" The sheriff's back was to them as they came in. He hung up the phone and turned to face them. "Well, Ms. Reed. I'm interested in how you'll try to explain this evidence away."

"I don't have anything to explain. But you do."

Colt touched her shoulder. "Can I put your things in a locker?" Caitlyn thrust her bag at him and he secured them for her. He then walked her to the jail cell and opened the door. "I'm sorry, Caitlyn." He said without looking her in the eye.

"Whatever, Colt. I knew I couldn't trust you." Her pulse beat war drums inside her skull.

Colt looked at her then, pain pulsing around his pupils.

"You *can* trust me, Catie. I promise I'll be by your side through this whole thing. No matter what we find." He stared into her eyes, which only enraged the flames of fury inside her head.

Caitlyn sat down on the cot and rested her face in her hands. She ran over what Colt had said this morning. *They have the slug that killed Wendy and its casing. The casing has my fingerprint on it—of course. And the bullet was fired from my gun...* Caitlyn gnawed on the lower corner of her lip as she thought. Distracted, she jumped to her feet. "Colt, you need to let the vet know I'm here. Please, find out what he has to say about Renegade."

Colt made the call to the veterinarian on his way out the door. Catie returned to her position on the cot, allowing her mind to wander once again through all the evidence that she knew about the murder. There were so many things they still didn't know. She tried to focus on those, but Sheriff Tackett approached the jail cell.

"I think your brother is in on this too, somehow. Before long, we'll have the both of you sent to prison for murder. You can't get away with this kind of thing in my county." Caitlyn glared at him as he walked over to the front door, reached for his hat and left.

Before long, Colt returned. He tried to smile, but failed. "Dr. Moore says he'd like to run a few more tests on Renegade. He's agreed to keep him at the clinic until you can pick him up. Whenever that is." He cast his gaze to the floor.

Caitlyn stood and gripped the bars of the cell. "Colt, look at me." Slowly, he raised his eyes to meet hers. "I did not have anything to do with Wendy's murder. There are too many holes in this case. Yesterday, after you left my place, I found another threat written in red marker on my bathroom sink. Whoever wrote it left a dead squirrel in my sink." She gripped a bar and pushed her forehead against it. "Someone slit my truck tire, left me two threatening notes, and a dead squirrel. Someone attacked me in my home. Someone wants me to stop investigating. That same someone is the real murderer."

"I agree with you. But the evidence... The Sheriff has enough to hold you this time, Catie. He thinks your attacker is your partner, trying to scare you into staying quiet."

"Oh, come on! There is other evidence and you have to weigh all of it equally!" She kicked at the door. "You say I can trust you. Okay, then I need you to get more information. I won't be able to do it, being stuck in here." Colt considered her but said nothing, so she continued. "First, you have to find out what happened when Jim took Wendy down to Sundance to that motel. Did she check in? Did Jim leave right away? Did he take her somewhere else? What did he do? If he left her there, where did he go? And can someone give him an alibi?" Caitlyn paced the floor in the cell as she spoke.

"I'll go down there and look into it. But the other big question is, where was Dylan?"

Caitlyn glared at him. "Dylan has an alibi—he just doesn't want to reveal the person he was with at this point. He will if he has to."

"And you believe him?"

"Without a doubt." Caitlyn resumed her pacing. "Someone has left me two threatening notes and attacked me and Renegade in my home. Why? Who was it? I think the answers to those questions are pivotal in this case, Colt. We can't forget them." She glowered at him and slowly, he nodded.

"That is true, but you have to be honest with yourself too, Catie. It could be Dylan."

"Are you kidding me?" It was a good thing there were bars between them, or she might have slapped him upside the head.

"No, when I saw him yesterday, he was favoring his arm. Could that be because Renegade bit him?"

His implication made her angry, but she wasn't one to turn away from evidence. Even the impossible to explain fact that her gun was the one that killed Wendy. She thought hard. "No, Dylan was at my house yesterday afternoon. He mentioned something about his shoulder hurting, but he said he'd taken a fall from his horse. He was wearing a T-shirt, and there were no bite marks that I could see. Whoever attacked me is going to have some serious torn flesh and bruising on their arm."

Colt took a step closer. "Well, that's something, then. Yesterday, we both noticed that Jim seemed injured, and also, the sheriff…"

"The sheriff what?" Caitlyn cocked her head.

"I doubt it's anything, but I bumped into him, and he winced."

Caitlyn shook her head and drew her overworked lip in between her teeth. She tasted blood and licked rather than chewed. "There's another thing that keeps running through my mind. Remember the day I gave you my Glock?"

"What about it?"

"Remember when I first released the magazine, it was fully loaded, right?"

Colt narrowed his eyes and nodded. "Yeah, I remember."

"And then, I removed the bullet I keep in the chamber. I always load my pistol that way, because it gives me an extra round. You remember that, right?"

Colt nodded, slowly at first, and then faster. "Yes, I do remember that."

Caitlyn's pulse darted erratically through her veins. She held Colt's gaze with the intensity of hers. "My gun was fully loaded, plus one, when I gave it to you. Is it still? I need you to check to see if the magazine is still holding the maximum number of rounds."

Colt swallowed hard, and his Adam's apple bobbed up and down his throat. His jaw muscles bulged as he turned and ran to the evidence room.

26

A flash of light cracked through the dismal gloom in his heart—through the hopelessness Colt had been carrying around with him all morning. If Catie was correct, the facts would implicate the sheriff. But looking into the evidence in this way could mean Colt's job if she was wrong. He prayed she was right, because then there was a chance they could have a future together. His heart beat so hard he had to blink three times to convince his eyes to focus on the log manifest. He lifted a clear plastic pouch and peered inside at the Glock's magazine. It was full—but where was the spare bullet Catie kept inside the firing chamber of her gun? He could hardly breathe.

A second bag held the slug that killed Wendy. In the third was the casing that had Caitlyn's fingerprint on it. He was absolutely certain there had been an extra round inside the chamber of Caitlyn's pistol. He remembered her removing it for him. His heart clanged against his ribs like an empty cup across jail bars.

Colt brought the bags of evidence out of the locker along with Caitlyn's 9mm Glock. He took them to the cell to show her. "Your magazine is full, but you were right. The round that was in your chamber is missing."

"This could change everything." Caitlyn reached out through the bars and pointed at the evidence bags. "Hold the one containing the slug up to the light." He did, and she studied it closely. "That doesn't look like it went through anyone's body to me."

"Sometimes, testing can destroy tissue evidence."

"Hmm. I guess the only way to know for sure is to have that slug re-tested for Wendy's DNA. Can you take it to the lab?"

Colt nodded. "I'll sign these bags out of the locker with a memo stating where they're going. We'll sort this out, one way or the other." Colt slipped the zip-closed bags into a large manila envelope.

"We don't have time to send them by certified courier. Can you drive them down?"

"Absolutely." Colt put on his deputy hat. "When the sheriff returns, tell him I went down to Cheyenne. I'll be back tomorrow." Colt opened the door.

"Wait!" Caitlyn gripped the bars. "After they test that slug for DNA, also have them recheck to be certain that it came from my gun."

"They already said it did."

"Just ask, okay?"

"Will do. I'm sorry I have to leave you here, Catie. I'll call your mom on my way out of Moose Creek. She'll make sure to feed you. If we find what we're hoping, you'll be out of that cell as soon as I get back."

"Don't bother my parents. You'll just worry them."

"They need to know, Catie, and you need their support."

True to his word, as he headed south, Colt called Reed Ranch. "Mrs. Reed, this is Deputy Branson. I'm calling to let you know Caitlyn is in jail at the Sheriff's Office."

"What are you talking about, Colt?"

"I don't have time to explain, I'm headed down to the crime lab in Cheyenne to check on some evidence. I'll be back tomorrow, early afternoon. But Caitlyn is going to need some decent food. She's called her attorney, and he's on the way. He'll make sure she has everything else she needs. But knowing Sheriff Tackett, he'll try to feed her dry bologna sandwiches. I thought maybe you'd like to bring her something more substantial than that. Plus, I'm betting she could use some support."

"I don't understand, Colt. Why is Caitlyn in jail? What did she do?" Stella's voice rang with alarm.

"It would probably be best if you went to the Sheriff's Office and talked to Catie about it yourself. I'll be back as soon as I can." Colt clicked off.

He glanced at the envelope on the passenger seat containing the precious evidence that could prove Catie's innocence... or her guilt. He desperately wanted to believe she had nothing to do with the murder. He couldn't imagine her killing anyone in cold blood. It didn't make sense—unless she was defending someone she loved... like Dylan. He shrugged the unhappy thought away and clicked on his flashing lights.

Colt took I-90 into Sundance. With a good amount of luck, if he hurried, he might be able to find the motel where Hague said he took Wendy the night she was killed. Jim claimed he didn't remember the name of the place, but fortunately Sundance was a small town.

As he drove down the main drag through town, Colt pulled into various motels along the way. At the first stop, he interrupted a soap opera the woman behind the desk was watching. She glanced back and forth between the photo he showed her of Wendy and the TV screen.

"I saw her face on the news. That's the woman who got

murdered up in Moose Creek, isn't it?" Her smoker's voice rose a notch with interest.

"Yes. Is it possible she checked in here on the night of Friday, May 14th?"

The woman grudgingly moved to the desktop computer and clicked several keys on the keyboard. "Nope. We had a family staying here at the time, and three singles—all male." She paused to watch a scene of her show.

Colt removed a business card from his shirt pocket and tapped its edge sharply on the counter to regain the clerk's attention. "If you remember anything else, or hear of anyone who might have seen her, will you please call me?"

She glared at his interruption. "Yeah, I'll call." Taking his card and tossing it onto the desk, she re-immersed herself in her daytime drama.

Colt drove to the next motel on the street. This one was more up-scale and the woman who greeted him when he entered was friendly and efficient, but she couldn't help him. Receiving her promise to call him if she learned anything, Colt was back on the road. The clock on the dashboard reminded him his time was short. He had to get to Cheyenne before the Crime Lab closed.

His next stop proved to be a complete bust, as construction workers had boarded it up for renovations. By the look of things, the building was ready to collapse any minute. He'd take one last look before he abandoned his motel investigation for the day. Another mile down the road he saw a sign for the "Mountain Lion Inn" and turned into the parking lot.

The man behind the desk in the lobby took Wendy's photo and ogled it. "Yeah. I remember her. Pretty thing. She was in here a week or so ago, I think." He blinked up at Colt. "You looking to arrest her for somethin'?"

The electric pulse of adrenaline snapped through Colt's

veins at his success in finding the right motel. "Was she with anyone else? Did someone come inside to register with her?"

The clerk scratched his chin and ran his tongue over chapped lips. "I don't think so. No."

Colt showed him recent snapshots of Dylan and Jim. "Have you ever seen either of these men before?"

The man sucked his teeth and shook his head. "Nope, can't say I have."

"How did the woman seem to you when she checked in, mood wise? Was she happy... sad... anything stand out to you? Maybe she'd been drinking?"

Frowning, the man thought. "She'd had a few, but she wasn't stumbling drunk, or anything. I can't say much about her mood. Maybe she seemed tired, a'course that's pretty common at a motel. She was quiet, but nothin' seemed wrong, if that's what you mean."

Colt leaned on the counter and peered at an ancient, boxy monitor. "Can you look up what kind of room she rented? Was it for a single or double?"

Rheumy eyes darted around the desktop before blinking up at Colt. "I didn't write any of that down."

"Don't you keep records on your computer?" Colt glanced at his watch. He didn't have time to drag information out of this guy.

"Well... if I remember correctly... she paid in cash." The man avoided looking him in the eye.

Colt figured the clerk didn't record Wendy's room rental so he could pocket the cash. "Are you sure there was no one with her? Did you see her car?"

"On second thought, I think there was a man in the car. He was driving, if memory serves."

"Can you describe him? Was he one of these men?" Colt held the photos up again.

The clerk shook his head in thought. "No. I couldn't

really see the driver with the motel lights glaring off the windshield."

"How about the make and model of the car?"

"The car was white—looked new—I think. I don't know what kind, though. Don't figure it's any of my business, you know?"

Colt didn't know. Most decent motels ask for their patron's type of car and their license plate number when they record their registration. "Do you have security cameras here?"

A rough smile split the man's face, and he chuckled. "We don't even have vending machines. The owner here is way too cheap for cameras."

"Okay, then, did you notice if she went straight to her room? Or did she go somewhere else first?"

"Pretty sure she went straight there. It's the door on the end." The man pointed out the window to a long brick building with a row of green doors. "At one point there was another car parked down there too. A small dark car."

"One that didn't belong to another customer?"

"No one else was renting a room on that side."

"Did she stay in her room all night?"

The clerk shrugged. "Not sure, but I got off at four in the morning, and it seems like I remember the parking lot being empty. Only reason I remember that, is 'cause it's not normal."

Colt thanked the man and handed him his card, just in case, though he assumed he'd never get a call. At this point, all he knew was the name of the motel Wendy had checked into, the fact that she was actually there, and that she was with someone—most likely a male, and possibly a third person. Hell, he wished he could talk to some other patrons who were there that night, but he had to get going. He wouldn't get anywhere pressing this guy for information about other guests without a warrant, anyway.

Back on the road toward Cheyenne, Colt realized he should have asked if the driver had a beard. Then he remembered the clerk mentioned the vehicle was a car... not a truck. Wendy's vehicle, a white Honda, was found ditched near the forest access road. He needed to find out who owned the smaller dark car.

Back on the highway, Colt drove over ninety miles an hour most of the way down to Cheyenne. He pulled into the crime lab parking lot just after three o'clock that afternoon. After signing in, he spoke to the investigator in charge, explaining the urgency of the situation. The supervisor agreed to perform a quick blood trace test on the slug Colt brought in. A full DNA test would take longer, but if what Colt suspected was true, he wouldn't need that. The forensic investigator promised to have results for him first thing the next day.

Fortunately, Colt's parents had friends who lived in Cheyenne, and he arranged to stay the night with them. He barely slept, tossing and kicking the covers. By eight in the morning, he was back at the lab.

The supervising tech invited him into his office. "There are some serious issues I'd like to discuss. First, we ran the bullet that you brought in yesterday through a chemical process. We sprayed the slug with Luminal and then studied it under a UV light. We found no traces of blood. In order to be certain, we put the slug through two further confirmatory tests. There was absolutely zero blood or tissue trace. I can, with confidence, confirm that this bullet never passed through any blood or organic tissue."

Colt's muscles went lax, and he gripped the desk for support. *Catie is innocent!* "Is there any way you can determine what the round hit?" Colt stared at the man's computer screen as though it was a Magic 8 Ball and could answer all his questions.

"It's possible. But that testing would take a lot longer and the results would be speculative. But if you like, we can run those tests next, since we don't need to do a DNA test." The tech leaned back in his chair and tapped his pen on the edge of his desk. "However, my greater concern is that the slug we tested in this case—the one brought in by the CSI—had plenty of trace evidence on it. I ran those tests myself and I remember." He narrowed his eyes at Colt and leaned forward. "I can tell you, with absolute certainty, this slug is not the same one that was originally tested."

Colt's ears rang with his words. "What?"

"This is not the same slug that I tested before. It appears someone has tampered with the evidence."

"Holy Christ." Colt wiped his mouth with the back of his hand as he grappled with the implication of what the scientist was saying. "Did you test the ballistics? Did this bullet come from the gun I left here with you?"

"Yes. This slug was fired from that specific gun—without a doubt. I can show you the markings if you like."

We've found the missing round. "Are you prepared to testify in court that this is not the slug that killed Wendy Gessler and that it is also not the same one that came to the lab originally?"

"Yes. In fact, we have photos of the original evidence." The tech slipped on a pair of gloves and lifted the bag the slug was in. "I don't know what is going on here, but even without comparing the photo to this slug, I am sure they are two different bullets."

"I'd like to leave this evidence here, signed over to you, so you can perform further testing, but will you please write up a report confirming that this bullet did not pass through anyone's skull."

The lab tech smiled confidently. "Yes, we are capable of finding trace evidence deep inside the folds of the metal, even after someone has tried to wash a bullet clean. I can assure you there's no way this round had that type of contact."

Colt lowered himself to the corner of the desk and cocked his head. "Can you tell me what you found on the slug the investigator brought here that indicated it was the one that killed Wendy Gessler?"

"Of course. The CSI submitted a 9mm slug she discovered in the dirt at the crime scene. There was blood, brain matter, and tissue found on that slug that all matched the DNA tags for Wendy Gessler. We also received soil samples that were tested for blood on site at the crime scene. After the field test showed blood splatter, we tested the dirt again and confirmed what the field tests hypothesized. We know the victim was shot at the gravesite, and by the splatter pattern we were able to determine that she was alive when she was shot."

"What evidence did you receive from Sheriff Tackett's office?"

"The only request Sheriff Tackett made on this case was ballistic testing. He sent us six rifles, a 9mm Glock 43 pistol, a spent 9mm slug, and a 9mm shell. We determined the slug was indeed fired from the accompanying Glock, and we found a partial fingerprint on the casing. I believe the round you brought in yesterday is that same slug."

"You weren't asked to do a DNA test on it?"

"No, just on the one brought in by the CSI. Sheriff Tackett only requested ballistics testing on this one."

Sudden clarity flashed through Colt's mind like a lightning bolt. *Oh, my God. There are two slugs! Tackett's trying to frame Caitlyn for Wendy's murder!* "Can you print out an inventory list of all the evidence you have processed for that crime?"

The tech leaned forward and typed on his keyboard. Documents appeared on the screen. He clicked on the print button and then faced Colt. "All other records of evidence are at the medical examiner's office, because they involve the victim's body."

Colt scanned the printout. "Let me make completely sure I understand. You tested two different bullets. One that killed Wendy Gessler, and this one, that has no trace of blood or tissue on it at all."

"Yes, sir. That is correct."

Colt's shock dissipated, replaced by elation, as the tech handed him the lab report printout. "Thanks so much for rushing this through." He paused only to shake the man's hand before he ran out of the building with the report. He jumped into his Jeep and drove as fast as he could back home.

He slowed down to the speed limit as he entered town, and it seemed as though he crawled through the streets. He couldn't wait to tell Caitlyn the fantastic news. He pictured how grateful she would be that he saved her from being falsely convicted of a crime. In his imagination, she jumped into his arms and kissed him. Tempted to allow that fantasy to swirl down a sultry path, Colt grinned and reminded himself he was driving. But surely, his actions would redeem him in her eyes. Catie would be so relieved he rescued her, that she would have to let his past mistakes go, and if he was lucky, they would have a lifelong future together.

It was midafternoon, and most people were inside or at work. So, it struck him as odd when he saw Jim Hague standing in Eleanor Smooter's front yard. The man was gesturing wildly and when Colt got closer; he realized Jim was yelling at a young pregnant woman who was standing on the lawn in front of him. Colt slowed his Jeep and rolled down his window. He started to ask if everything was all right, when the woman hauled off and smacked Hague in the arm with her purse. Colt did a double take when he heard the man yowl in pain. Jim clutched his shoulder and fell to his knees.

Colt was about to pull over when the woman marched up the front porch steps and Jim remained seated on the lawn. It looked to him like the minor spat had ended and it was far more important to get the lab documents to the jail. Besides, it appeared the woman handled the situation fine on her own. Colt would force Sheriff Tackett to release Caitlyn, and then, after he basked in the joy of her gratitude, he would return to check on Jim.

27

Caitlyn and her attorney had the Sheriff's office to themselves. They ate sandwiches her mom had brought in as they went over every detail of the case that Caitlyn was aware of. She also shared the timeline of events she had compiled. "The one thing I couldn't figure out, was how my gun could possibly be the murder weapon."

Mr. Vanderbilt, the attorney Logan had recommended, took notes on a yellow legal pad. He scratched a few more words on the lined paper before looking up at her. "You're certain no one knows your gun safe combination, or that your safe wasn't tampered with in any way?"

"My dad has the combo, but he'd never give it to anyone."

"Was it written down? Perhaps someone found the combination?"

"I suppose that's possible, but whoever that might be still had to get inside my truck. None of this made any sense to me until the deputy brought out the evidence bags yesterday morning." Caitlyn stood and shook the tension out of her arms. "The sheriff didn't send the slug or casing to the crime lab until after Deputy Branson confiscated all the guns from my family's ranch. Shouldn't he have sent those in right away?"

"That will certainly be in my line of questioning. I'm wondering why he removed that evidence from the crime scene in the first place. It should have remained where it was for the CSI team to gather. The sheriff never should have separated it from the evidence they found at the scene. He's going to have to answer for that."

"Exactly, but even more interesting than that is the only piece of evidence Sheriff Tackett found and removed was a bullet casing. Deputy Branson told me the CSI found the bullet that passed through Wendy's skull and she took it with all the other evidence to the lab."

"Are you saying there are two bullets in evidence?"

"There are two bullets, but only one of them is in evidence." Caitlyn waited for the implication of what she said to filter into her attorney's mind.

"You have proof of this?" A sly gleam sparkled in his eye.

"I hope to as soon as Deputy Branson gets back from the state crime lab." Caitlyn chewed on her lip. "This mishandling of evidence should get me out of jail, right?"

"It will when—"

The front door of the Sheriff's Office flew open and crashed against the wall behind it, causing both Caitlyn and her attorney to jump.

"Catie!" Colt ran into the room waving some papers. "I took the slug and casing down to the crime lab in Cheyenne like you asked. I had them re-run the blood trace tests, and you won't believe what they found!"

"There are two different slugs, right?" Caitlyn's pulse surged with such force when she gripped the bars she felt as though she might bend them.

Colt blinked at her, momentarily stunned and slightly deflated. "Yeah. The slug that came from your gun didn't kill anyone at all. In fact, it has never come in contact with blood of any kind. There is no trace of blood or tissue to be found on it at all. But how did you know?"

Caitlyn stared at him, her mind churning. "It's the only thing that made sense." She paced the small cell before remembering to introduce Colt to her lawyer. The men shook hands. "Did you find out anything in Sundance?"

"Yes. I figured out which motel Wendy rented a room from. The guy at the desk remembered her and thinks she arrived in a white car with a man driving. At one point, he noticed another small dark car parked in front of her room. But when he got off work at four in the morning, neither car was in the lot."

"Did he describe the man? Or see anyone else?"

"No. I showed him pictures of both Jim and Dylan, but he said he didn't see anyone clearly."

Caitlyn's attorney gestured to the cell door. "Given the new evidence, can you—"

"Yeah." Colt rushed to the cell with his keys and unlocked the door. "That bullet may have come from your gun, but it didn't kill Wendy. We don't have the evidence to keep you in jail, so I'm letting you go."

Caitlyn wanted to speculate as to what the sheriff's motive was behind his mishandling of the evidence, but she put that aside for the time being. Thrilled to be free, she threw her good arm around Colt's neck and hugged him tight. "Thank you, so much for driving all the way down there. I needed proof before I could confront Tackett."

He pulled her in tight to his chest, their heart beats joining in tempo. "I'm just relieved to know you're innocent," he murmured into her hair.

His words slapped her like a cold drink tossed in her face. Caitlyn pushed back and narrowed her eyes. She raised her right brow. "It would've been nice if you believed in me *without* the evidence." Colt's cheeks grew ruddy as she withdrew her arm and turned away from him.

When Colt spoke again, excitement no longer buoyed his voice and the light in his eyes had dimmed. "I saw something curious on my way back into town," he lifted the lid on the copy machine. Pressing a few buttons, he copied the lab documents. He handed one set to Caitlyn's attorney and left a second stack on the sheriff's desk. "Jim Hague was in Eleanor Smooter's front yard, yelling at a pregnant woman I've never seen before."

"That must be Maribel. She's the woman I met with Eleanor at the Mercantile—Eleanor's houseguest." Caitlyn gathered her things. "What was he yelling at her about?"

"I don't know, but it was kind of funny." Caitlyn and her attorney waited for Colt to continue. "The lady—Maribel—apparently didn't like him screaming at her and responded to his verbal abuse by walloping him in the shoulder with her purse."

"Serves him right," Caitlyn chuffed.

"I agree, but then Hague cried out in pain and fell to the ground holding his arm." He raised his brows. "What do you make of that? I mean, he's a pretty big guy to get hurt so easily."

"Are they still there?" Caitlyn ran to the door.

The attorney slid the lab document and his notepad into his briefcase. "I'll let you two settle the local domestic dispute. I'm heading over to my B&B. I'd like to meet with you again to discuss your case before I head back to Denver, Caitlyn. How about tomorrow morning at nine o'clock?"

"Sounds good. I'll meet you at the cafe." Caitlyn hollered over her shoulder as she ran toward Colt's Jeep. "Come on Deputy, let's go see a man about a painful arm."

As Caitlyn and Colt ran to his Jeep, someone called out to Caitlyn from down the street.

"Caitlyn! Caitlyn, wait a minute."

She stopped in her tracks and turned toward the voice calling her name. Dr. Moore walked up the street in their direction with Renegade next to him on a leash. The vet waved and smiled as he rushed toward them.

"Running into you is a lucky coincidence. I have good news. I'm giving Renegade the all clear. There's no more bleeding in his brain."

Caitlyn fell to her knees and threw her good arm around her dog. "Oh buddy, I'm so glad to hear you're okay." Tears of joy moistened her cheeks and Renegade licked them away, slathering her face with his tongue. His tail swept back and forth excitedly.

"When I retested this morning, everything looked fine. Even the swelling has gone. I thought I'd take him on a walk and get him a little fresh air." The doctor quirked his lips. "The truth is, Renegade has been whining for you all day. I kept him sedated yesterday, and through the night. But I can't justify continuing the medication when he's doing so well."

Caitlyn peered up at the doctor. "Can I take him home, then?"

"You sure may. Most of the glass splinters were superficial. He has one gash on the side of his left front paw that I had to stitch up, but as you can see his pads aren't causing him pain. He shouldn't have any trouble walking." Dr. Moore patted Renegade's shoulder. "He probably has a headache, and I've prescribed some pain relievers for that and for the incisions. He's also on an antibiotic to prevent any infection, but he'll be happier and far more comfortable at home than he would be at the clinic."

Caitlyn rose to her feet and hugged the doctor. "Thank you so much, Dr. Moore. He couldn't have been in better hands."

"I'm glad it all turned out as well as it did. Renegade is a wonderful dog, and he obviously loves you."

"He sure is, and the feeling is mutual." Caitlyn stroked Renegade's face once more before she opened the back door to the Jeep for him. She sat in the front. "Come on, Colt. Let's go find Jim."

By the time they drove to Eleanor's, Jim and Maribel were sitting next to each other on the front porch steps. Jim pushed himself up to his feet when he saw Colt pull up to the curb.

"I drove by a little while ago and saw you two arguing," Colt said as he stepped out of his car. "I wanted to check and make sure everything was okay. What was the problem?"

Hague puffed himself up and took a threatening step toward Colt. "There's nothing going on here, Deputy. Nothing that's any of your business, anyway." The big man glowered down at Colt, his large hands curling into fists.

Caitlyn opened the back door and let Renegade out on his lead. Jim's eyes darted toward the dog, and he stepped back. Renegade barked at the man's sudden movement, and Caitlyn held her fist out in a silent command for her dog to sit.

Colt offered his hand to the pregnant woman. "Hi ma'am. I'm Deputy Branson, and you must be Maribel Martin?"

Cautiously, Maribel shook his hand and answered, "Yes, that's me."

"I want to make sure you're all right." Colt turned to Jim. "She must have hit you pretty hard. The pain brought you to your knees."

"You're mistaken, Deputy. I wasn't in any pain." Jim glared at Colt.

Renegade's chest rumbled with an ominous growl as he stretched to the end of his leash. The skin underneath Jim's tattooed neck flushed, but the color drained from his angry face.

"*Stuj*." Caitlyn commanded Renegade to stand, but when she released her tight grip on his lead, he lunged forward half a stride. Jim stepped back, his eyes shifting from Renegade to Colt and back. "Get that rabid monster away from me," he growled.

Colt spoke in a friendly tone. "I'm wondering, Hague, if we looked at your arm, would we find bite marks?"

Jim sneered. "If that dog tries to bite me, I'll break his mangy neck."

"Hague, were you out at Caitlyn's house two nights ago?" Colt crossed his arms. "Think before you answer. Honesty and cooperation go a long way."

Jim glared at him. "Why would I go to Caitlyn's house? She murdered my girlfriend."

Maribel pulled herself to her feet. "Stop calling that bitch your girlfriend. She was just some woman trying to trick you into marrying her."

"Shut your mouth, Maribel." Jim turned his venom on her.

"Why should I? That's what you told me."

"You're no better." Jim's muscles tensed and the chords in his neck stood out. "Look at you." He glowered at her in disgust.

Renegade barked and snarled, backing Jim up against the front wall of the house with his threatening posture. His lip curled and his fangs glistened in the sunshine.

"How dare you? You said you loved me." Maribel circled her belly protectively with her arms. Tears dripped from her eyes. "I would have done anything for you. I already have!"

"Shut your stupid mouth!" Jim's eyes darted from Renegade to Maribel and back. His rapid pulse evident in the throbbing veins at his temples.

"What have you done, Maribel?" Caitlyn asked softly. She studied the pregnant woman's face. She still couldn't shake the feeling that she recognized her from somewhere.

The woman broke down then. She lowered herself to the lawn and dropped her face into her hands, sobbing. "Oh, God…"

Jim snarled at her. "You'll be responsible for what happens if you keep talking."

"Are you threatening Maribel, Hague?" Colt stepped between them.

Caitlyn cocked her head. "Like you threatened me?"

"I never threatened you." Jim's flat slate eyes shot to her and she shivered at the hate she saw in them.

Colt rested his hand on the butt of his gun. "Did either of you have anything to do with Wendy's murder?"

"Jimmy, don't say another word without an attorney present," Maribel cried.

"Shut the hell up, woman!"

Caitlyn's mind worked furiously to connect the dots and figure out how she knew Maribel, what was going on, and how it all fit together. "Who owns that Toyota?" She pointed to the car parked at the curb.

Jim and Maribel both gawked at her as though she'd asked them to dance around naked with her sudden change of topic.

"Yeah, I haven't seen that car around Moose Creek before." Colt turned a speculative gaze to Maribel. "Does it belong to you, ma'am?"

"Yes, it's mine. What of it?" The pregnant woman sniffled and rested her arms on top of her rounded belly.

"We may need to impound it as evidence." Colt walked back across the lawn and crouched down by the front end of her car and studied it as he spoke. "You see, the night of Wendy's murder, a car just like this one sped out of the forest and clipped the corner of Caitlyn's truck about a mile east of the Reed Ranch road. Your Toyota, coincidentally, has a smashed front quarter panel and scrapes of paint that correspond with such a collision. You wouldn't know anything about that, would you?"

"Lots of cars have dented front ends. I had an accident several months ago, and I just haven't had it fixed yet." Maribel's eyes darted to Jim, who narrowed his eyes and shook his head.

"That's interesting, because your car has silver paint on it that is the same color as Caitlyn's truck. The crime lab can tell us if it's exactly the same paint, or not." Caitlyn took in the effect Colt's words had on Maribel. Her face reddened, but she didn't answer.

Colt shifted to include Jim in the next piece of information. "Recently, I found tire tracks on the top of the ridge near where Wendy's body was discovered. The tracks run along the BLM side of the fence line, coincidently at the top of the same rarely used forest access road. The imprints have been cast and we'll check them against the tires on your car, Ms. Martin."

Maribel's jaw dropped open, but she snapped it closed quickly and flashed an angry glare at Jim. "That was the night you borrowed my car."

"You were with me, Maribel. Don't try to pretend like you weren't." Renegade barked, not liking Jim's tone. Jim's focus switched from Maribel to Renegade. "I told you to call your damn dog off." Caitlyn had a firm hold on Renegade's leash, but that didn't seem to ease Jim's apprehension.

"I don't know what you're talking about, Jim." Maribel stomped up the porch steps. "That was the night you told me you were going to end things with your *other* girlfriend."

"Don't you dare try to put all this on me!"

Maribel spread her arms wide, including everyone in her

speech. "Jim was cheating on me with Wendy! I got pregnant seven months ago, and Jim promised to leave her and marry me. But he never did."

"Fucking women. You're all the same." Jim's distaste flowed from his expression to include both Maribel and Caitlyn.

"I don't know, Jim. Maybe you shouldn't have been double dipping in the first place!" Maribel shrieked. "You told me you'd convince your whore to have an abortion and then you'd be free to marry me." She turned her blotchy face to Colt. "He told me she would never let him go. That there was only one way."

"God damn it, Maribel. Shut your fat mouth!"

"You shut up! I saw you in the motel! Sure as hell didn't look like you wanted to be free of her!"

Caitlyn spared a glance toward Colt. He barely bobbed his head. If they remained quiet, they might find out everything. Caitlin popped Renegade's leash to settle him and take some pressure off of Hague.

"I was trying to convince the stupid bitch not to kill herself."

"Oh, that's rich. You should have just let her. That would have solved everything."

The vicious argument drew Caitlyn in. "How can you say such things?" Hot flames ignited in the pit of her belly. Anger flared at the accusations made about her brother, and her heart broke for the innocent baby Wendy had carried. "Wendy loved you, Jim. Maybe, Wendy and Dylan got together behind your back, but how does that make her any worse than you? Sleeping with two women at once?"

"Yeah!" Maribel yelled.

Jim glowered at Maribel, and evil tendrils curled through his words. "If you don't shut your fat face, I'll shut it for you," he hissed—spittle flying toward her. "This whole thing was your idea. You're the one who came up with the plan to kill Wendy."

Maribel's mouth opened and closed like a carp.

Tires squealed on the road behind them, and the acrid scent of burnt rubber filled the air. Everyone turned to see a car screeching to a stop in the middle of the street.

28

Sheriff Tackett jumped out of his Jeep. "Deputy Branson, what in the hell is going on here?"

"Sir, I believe we've found Wendy Gessler's murderers," he answered.

Tackett's complexion turned a sickly green as he scanned the scene. "Caitlyn Reed should be in jail. How did she get out?"

"Caitlyn is not the murderer. I think you know that." Colt cautiously stepped toward Hague. He reached to the back of his service belt to unclip his handcuffs. "Jim here, has basically confessed to the crime, and it appears that Maribel Martin is his partner."

"I don't know what kind of tale Ms. Reed is spinning, but she's completely suckered you in." Sheriff Tackett strode into the yard. "You're lucky I don't fire you, Deputy. You had no authority to release Ms. Reed from jail."

"I beg to differ, sir. I don't believe you had enough evidence—or any actual evidence at all—to hold her. In fact, her attorney didn't think so either." Colt clicked one side of his handcuffs around Jim's wrist. When he gripped Hague's shoulder, the man cried out.

The front door of the house swung open, and Eleanor Smooter stepped out onto the porch and she ran down the stairs. She flung her arm around Maribel's shoulders protectively. "What on earth is going on out here? You all are making enough noise to raise the dead." Her face paled and her eyes darted to Jim. "I'm sorry, unfortunate choice of words."

"Go back inside, Ellie." Tackett ordered.

"I will not. Don't start telling me what to do, Bruce. What is everyone doing out here?" Eleanor's firm chin jutted forward.

Colt cuffed the wrist of Jim's injured arm and sat him down on the porch steps.

Caitlyn murmured, "*Sedni*," and Renegade sat down but never took his menacing golden eyes off of Jim.

Colt rested his hands on his hips and glared at the sheriff. "Seems like Hague has a torn-up shoulder. Like he was attacked by a dog or something. But you knew that, didn't you, Sheriff?"

"You don't believe that bunch of nonsense, do you Deputy?" Tackett barked out a laugh. "That's exactly why you'll never make a good lawman. You're too gullible." Sheriff Tackett stepped forward. "You'd believe anything Caitlyn Reed told you, wouldn't you?"

Anger sparked in Colt's eyes. "I took the slug you had locked in the evidence locker down to the state crime lab yesterday. I'm betting you already know what they had to say," Colt challenged.

"I saw your doctored reports on my desk, if that's what you mean." Tackett countered.

Colt continued. "But what I can't figure out is why you would want to help these two get away with murder? Why you'd help to pin the crime on innocent people?"

Eleanor whispered something in Maribel's ear and before anyone could stop her, she darted back inside her house.

"I know for sure that bullet came from Caitlyn's gun. Either she shot Wendy, or Dylan did, but one of them killed Wendy Gessler with that gun." The sheriff pointed an accusing finger in Caitlyn's face.

Caitlyn slapped his hand away. "You mishandled that evidence, Sheriff. You know I had nothing to do with Wendy's murder. I—"

The front door flung open, and Eleanor rushed out, armed with a shotgun. She cocked it. The familiar chuck-chick sound sent tremors through Caitlyn's body. In the split second of distraction, Sheriff Tackett sprang. He threw an arm around Caitlyn's neck and pulled her backward into a choke hold, his arm folded like a vice squeezing her neck. Eleanor fired the shotgun. By the time the echo from the explosion faded, Caitlyn was losing the battle for consciousness. She wriggled and bucked, trying to get loose from Tackett's tightening hold. As she fought for breath, she realized Tackett was pressing the muzzle of his gun into her temple. Renegade growled and snapped.

"Nobody move!" The sheriff yelled. "Tell your damn dog to back off or I'll shoot his brains all over the yard."

"*Lehne*, Ren." Caitlyn choked out. He snarled and lunged toward them. Tackett pressed the gun hard into her bruised head. "*Lehne!*" she screamed. Renegade's eyes met hers. They were wild with fury, but he obeyed her.

Colt held up his hands. "Everyone, calm down."

Tackett glared at Jim and Maribel. "I never should've got involved in this. I tried to help you, but now look at the mess you've gotten all of us into."

Caitlyn rallied all her remaining strength and jerked her

body to the side. *"Drz!"* The command scraped across her crushed vocal chords, but it was enough. Renegade went ballistic. All fangs, fur, and fury he flew through the air. Caitlyn's vision dimmed from lack of oxygen, but she heard Sheriff Tackett scream in her ear.

Someone yelled, "Daddy!"

A second shotgun blast assaulted the air, and Caitlyn fell to the ground.

COLT DOVE AT ELEANOR, knocking the older woman to the wooden porch. He grasped the shotgun and yanked it from her hands as he sought out Caitlyn. He leapt down the steps in one bound, horrified at the sight of Caitlyn's limp form crumpled on the grass. "Caitlyn!" he yelled. *Where had Eleanor aimed the second shotgun blast? Was Caitlyn shot? Catie, please!*

Renegade pinned Tackett to the ground, his teeth buried in the man's neck and shoulder. He tossed his head back and forth, yanking and growling, tearing flesh and tendons. The sheriff's screams communicated his excruciating pain. Every time Tackett attempted to move, Renegade tugged on him again, plunging his bite deeper. Tackett wailed in agony.

Colt skidded to Caitlyn's side on his knees and brushed long strands of her hair out of her face. Gripping her shoulder, he prepared himself to attend to a wound seeping blood. Gently, he rolled her toward him. Caitlyn's face was a ghostly white, making the bruise on her temple garish. Her lips were tinged blue. Colt felt her neck for a pulse.

"Catie?"

29

Caitlyn blinked. Coughing, she tried to push herself up. Colt drew her into his chest. "Thank, God. Were you hit?" He held her away to check her over, tracing her face with his fingertips.

"No. I'm okay." Slowly, she regained her equilibrium, and then pushed herself up on her hands and knees. Young green shoots pressed up through the cold dead grass, softening the turf below her. Colt helped her to her feet. She ran her fingers over her sore larynx.

Maribel was on her knees pleading. "Let him go!"

"Tackett," she rasped. "I'm going to ask Renegade to release you, but he'd love nothing more than to rip your throat out, so I suggest you don't move. Understand?" Caitlyn coughed, her tender throat thickening. She hoped Tackett hadn't damaged her trachea. She gaped at Maribel. "Did I hear you call him, Daddy?"

Maribel wept into her hands. The sheriff gritted his teeth. "Just get him off me!"

"Renegade, *Pust.*" Without letting go, her dog looked up at her from the top of his eyes as if checking to see that she meant what she said. *"Pust!"* Caitlyn repeated, the word scraping her hoarse voice.

Renegade released Tackett's shoulder, but stood poised next to his head, baring his teeth and emitting a menacing growl. Caitlyn gave Colt a weak smile and whispered. "He's not going anywhere." She knelt down and unclipped the sheriff's handcuffs from his belt and tossed them to Colt. "Why don't you put these on Maribel... Tackett? And use your spare pair on Eleanor."

Caitlyn glanced at Jim, but he hadn't moved from his seated position on the steps. His chin rested on his chest, and his shoulders slumped in defeat. Caitlyn stared down at Maribel. "I'm guessing you and Jim murdered Wendy and when I found her body, you went to your dad—the Sheriff—to get help covering up the crime?"

Maribel spat at her in response.

Caitlin wiped her cheek with the back of her hand. "Nice. You know, I thought I recognized you. But now I see that you just reminded me of someone." She turned to Tackett. "You."

She took the young woman by the arm. "I'll lock Maribel and Eleanor in the back seat of the sheriff's car for now." She considered the man on the porch steps. Even though in her mind he deserved every bit of the pain he was in, she knew that his wounds could get infected and ultimately kill him. Caitlyn lifted her chin and gave Colt a brave face. "You ought to call an ambulance for these two."

With each new breath, Caitlyn gained strength. She marched the women to the sheriff's Jeep and helped them into the back. "Looks like you'll be having this baby in prison," she said to Maribel.

"What will happen to it?"

"If you're convicted, they'll place your baby with your next of kin."

Maribel's dark eyes widened. "There is no one. It's just me and my dad."

"Then, they'll have to put the baby in foster care. Unless, you do the selfless thing and allow for an adoption."

Tears coursed down Maribel's face. "I only wanted to keep Jim. Now, I'm losing everything."

Caitlyn nodded and closed the locked door. She had no sympathy to offer the woman who murdered her unborn niece or nephew and its mother.

Renegade's presence kept Tackett pinned to the ground, while Colt called the medical clinic. "We need paramedics at The Smooter's residence on Third Street, right away."

HE HELPED Jim to his feet and escorted him down the steps. "Hell of an afternoon, huh?" He grimaced at Caitlyn. "Good thing Ms. Smooter has horrible aim."

"No kidding. As soon as the paramedics get here, Renegade and I will take the women to jail."

Colt ran his tongue over his teeth. "I guess after I arrest Tackett, then I automatically become the acting sheriff."

"Sounds about right." Caitlyn held out her hand. "Give me your handcuff key. I'll need it at the jail."

"So, if I'm the new sheriff," Colt dropped the key into her palm. "Then, I'll need to make you a deputy so that you'll have the authority to lock those women up."

Caitlyn stopped in her tracks and turned back to Colt. "Seriously? What do you have to do to make it official?"

"Nothing really, just say something like, 'Caitlyn Reed, I officially deputize you to assist me in carrying out and enforcing the law in Moose Creek County.'"

"Awesome. Can I wear your deputy badge?" She grinned at him and his knees wavered.

Locking the joints so he wouldn't stumble, Colt snickered. "You can wear the extra one in my desk, if you want." He watched her walk back to the sheriff's car. *No deputy I've ever known wore their jeans quite as well as this one does.* He couldn't manage to wipe the grin from his face.

Tackett growled, "Stop gawking at that woman and help me up."

Colt glanced down at the injured man. "You no longer have any authority to tell me what to do, Tackett, and I don't think Renegade is going to let you move until the paramedics get here."

"Make her call him off."

"Something tells me nobody *makes* Caitlyn Reed do anything." Colt left Tackett under Renegade's capable watch and made his way over to Jim. The siren of an old station-wagon style ambulance drifted on the breeze. "Come on. Let's get you taken care of."

Jim rose to his feet, but winced when Colt gripped his shoulder.

"Mind if I have a look?" Colt gestured at Jim's arm.

The man shrugged and looked away, so Colt pulled open his shirt and slid the fabric over Jim's shoulder. Colt sucked a quick gulp of air. Bruised skin and torn, inflamed flesh surrounded obvious bite marks on Jim's arm. The angry red wounds oozed and already streaking with infection.

Colt grimaced. "Didn't you go to the doctor?"

Jim shrugged with his good shoulder. "I didn't want to have to answer any questions."

"If this were to get infected, it could give you blood poisoning—which could kill you."

"Might be better to die that way, than to spend the rest of my life in jail."

Colt shook his head with incredulity. "Maybe if you thought about that ahead of time, you'd have been smart enough not to murder someone. Come on." He took Jim by his good arm and led him down to the edge of the lawn to wait for medical assistance.

Caitlyn waved to him from the Jeep. "As acting deputy, I just called the sheriff in Gillette. They have room for Hague and Tackett as soon as they're released from the clinic. Stay at the facility with those two and don't take your eyes off either of them."

Caitlyn's assertive demeanor took Colt back for a second, but he responded to her, grinning. "Yes, ma'am."

Caitlyn nodded and called Renegade to her side. Together, the woman he loved and her dog jumped into the front seat of the sheriff's car and drove away like they owned it. Colt chuckled under his breath. Maybe he'd hire her on as his deputy full-time once he was officially the new sheriff.

30

By the end of the following week, Caitlyn and Colt had completed processing the murderers and their accomplices along with typing up the complete investigation. The four suspects were in various county jails awaiting their official indictments and trials.

Finally, Caitlyn enjoyed a much-deserved day off. She smirked to herself as she made the last turn into her family's ranch. *As if working cattle is a day off.*

Caitlyn reached over and ruffled the fur on Renegade's head. "Ready to chase some cows?" She opened the door and hopped out of the truck, and Renegade leapt to the ground behind her.

Dylan strode out of the barn and smiled at her. It occurred to her how handsome her oldest brother was when he wasn't scowling. He raised a hand to wave. "About time you got here. Half the day is over already."

"Whatever." She laughed. "Let me get Whiskey saddled up and we're all ready to go."

"I appreciate the help." Dylan checked the cinch on Sampson's saddle.

"No problem, Dyl. I'm happy to be here." Caitlyn went into the barn to tack up her horse. It was good to be on speaking terms with her brother again after so many long months of animosity.

Together, they rode out to the farthest pasture. It was time to round up the herd and move them up to the BLM for summer grazing. Caitlyn and her brother rode side-by-side with Renegade scampering along behind them. She gazed at Dylan's profile for a moment before she asked, "So, how are you doing?"

It took a while before he responded. "Did I tell you I offered to marry Wendy when she told me she was pregnant?"

"No, but it doesn't surprise me. That's the kind of man you are."

Dylan glanced at her from the corner of his eye. "She said no. She told me she loved Jim and didn't want to marry me, but that Jim wanted her to have an abortion." Dylan sighed. "I tried to talk her out of it. I begged her not to do it. But I guess men don't have any choice about the lives of their unborn babies in these situations." He was quiet for several strides. "You know, looking back, she seemed afraid of making Hague angry."

"And now we know why."

"Yeah."

They rode in silence for a minute. "I'm really sorry, Dylan."

"I told her I would raise the baby if she didn't want it. But nothing I said mattered to her. I don't know why she bothered to tell me. I kinda wish she didn't, because now I have this hole in my heart."

Caitlyn couldn't find the words to say. *Still waters really do run deep.*

Dylan chuffed. "I didn't even know I wanted kids. But now, it's all I can think about."

"Well, it's going to be hard to meet someone if you never leave the ranch." Caitlyn teased, hoping to lighten the mood.

Her brother chuckled. "I suppose that's true enough."

"I have Saturday off. Let's go out. Me and you. It'll be fun!"

Dylan flashed her a skeptical look. "Now you want to take me wife shopping? I think I can handle that on my own."

"I doubt it. You've done a pretty crappy job of it so far."

"Hey, now." Dylan gathered his reins. "Race you to the gate." He closed his legs around his horse, and they bolted forward.

Caitlyn laughed and did the same, knowing she and Whiskey would never catch up to them with Dylan's head start.

Her brother leaned down and unlatched the double gate that opened to the BLM. As one unit, Dylan and Sampson maneuvered the panels open before both riders circled the herd. Dylan tracked to the left and Caitlyn and Renegade turned to the right, gradually pushing the cows towards the open gate. Renegade surprised her, acting like a trained shepherd, instinctively herding the cows. It wasn't long before the lead cows realized they were being guided toward open pasture and started gamboling toward the gate. By the end of the hour, Caitlyn and Dylan were securing the gate to the summer pasture and turning for home.

"I have some good news for you." Caitlyn nudged her brother's leg with her boot as they rode side by side.

"I could sure use some of that."

"You know I've been working as Colt's deputy for the past week."

"Yeah?"

"Well, he offered me the job for real, as soon as I go

through the Wyoming Law Enforcement Academy. I think I've finally found work I love." She laughed. "And of course I enjoy the paycheck, too."

"About time you got a real job." Dylan smirked at her. "You're a terrible waitress."

"Shut up." She laughed. "I didn't really need a steady job before. My place is paid for in full. I was managing fine on the cash I earned at the café and from what I had left over after buying my cabin. I don't have a car payment, and I haven't even been on the hook to feed my horse."

"Oh, you'll be getting my bill." Dylan winked.

"Good. That's only right. But listen, I have an idea." Caitlyn sat back in her saddle, and Whiskey slowed to a stop. Dylan turned to her in question and halted Sampson. Caitlyn stared directly into Dylan's eyes. "I'm going to use my paycheck every month to pay the mortgage on this ranch. At least until we have a good market year for the cows."

Dylan blinked at her, unable to speak. He swallowed several times. His eyes grew moist, and he scrunched his brows. He ground his teeth against his obvious emotion.

"It's the right thing to do. I want to do it. And I'm *going* to do it. Okay?" Caitlyn held her breath.

Dylan nodded once and turned his horse toward home. Caitlyn understood. If he spoke, he'd reveal his feelings, and that would never do. Not for Dylan. Caitlyn smiled to herself and nudged Whiskey to take her home. Renegade trotted through the fields in front of the horses, leading the way.

Monday morning, Colt was the first to arrive at the Sheriff's Office. He was still getting used to taking his position behind the main desk, but he liked how it felt to be the one in charge. He settled into the big leather chair and leaned back, propping his feet on the corner of the work surface. He heard Caitlyn's voice calling out to Renegade, and he smiled as she came in through the front door.

"Good morning, Deputy." Colt grinned at her.

Caitlyn smiled back. "Good morning, Sheriff."

Hearing his new title and greeting his beautiful new deputy would never get old. "You're here just in time. I wanted to go over all the case details with you and make sure we haven't missed anything."

"Okay." Caitlyn hung her cowboy hat on the rack.

"Eleanor Smooter, faces charges as an accessory to murder after the fact. Even though she had little to do with the crime, she knew about it. She'll also be charged with assault with a deadly weapon. I don't know what kind of sentence she's looking at, but she could face up to fifteen years." Colt closed the file he was referring to and opened the next one. "Bruce Tackett, on the other hand, is in big trouble. His charges will include accessory to murder after the fact, along with, interfering with an investigation, conspiring to robbery and assault, and assault with a deadly weapon. If he's convicted for all those charges, he'll be going to prison for at least twenty years, and as you know, lawmen don't do well in prison."

Caitlyn filled a bowl with water for Renegade and set it next to her desk. He lapped it up like he was dying of thirst, splashing all over the floor. She pulled out her chair and sat. "I gather both Maribel and Jim are being charged with first-degree murder?"

Colt tapped a pen on his desk. "Yes, though it was Jim who actually pulled the trigger while Maribel held Wendy. Poor girl, with the Rohypnol in her system, Wendy didn't even know what was happening to her."

Caitlyn shook her head. "The whole situation is terribly sad. Wendy was so upset over the fact that she was pregnant and that Jim was going to leave her, she felt like she wanted to die. But she didn't mean it. She was just scared and depressed. I can't believe Jim used that as an excuse to solve his problems—that he thought the easiest way out of his mess was to kill Wendy."

"It's tragic."

"No kidding. It's pure evil. I can't believe Maribel manipulated her dad into covering up a murder."

"Yeah, but when I talked to him, he intimated that Jim threatened to hurt his daughter and the baby if he didn't help them."

"I guess it shows how far a parent will go to protect a child."

Colt lowered his feet from the desk and sat forward in his chair. "Jim was stupid though—trying to attack you with

Renegade around." His fingers responsively curled into fists at the thought of the man's hands on Caitlyn.

"Both he and Tackett are complete idiots if they thought they could get away with trying to hurt me." She reached down and scratched her dog behind the ears. "Isn't that right, buddy?" He licked her hand in response.

Caitlyn looked up at Colt with a broad smile spread across her face. "You should've seen him, flying through my living room window, shattering the glass to save me. It was a terrifyingly awesome sight."

"He's an exceptional dog." One he owed an enormous debt of gratitude to.

"For sure. He's wicked smart and his instincts are dead on, but he needs some work on discipline." She got up and moved around to the front of her desk to lean against the corner. "And frankly, I need some training too—if we want to be a sharp K-9 police team, that is."

"I love the idea of having our very own K-9 unit in our little department."

Caitlyn's smile was radiant. "I found a trainer online. She lives in Florida, and trains police dogs for a living. Normally, I'd have to send my dog to her for several weeks, but she's attending a competition in Utah next month. And since Ren just needs some fine tuning, she's agreed to come and stay with me for a week or two on her way home for a training intensive—as long as I provide her with room and board."

"Sounds great."

"Yeah. I'm hoping there's money for training in our budget." Caitlyn smiled but soon was tugging on the corner of her bottom lip with her teeth. "Colt, there are still a couple of things bothering me about the murder case."

"Like what?" Colt opened the file on his desk and looked down at the paperwork he thought was ready to put away.

"Well, Tackett explained how he'd fired my gun at the

range and then exchanged that slug and its casing for the ones found at the crime scene. But whatever happened to the actual evidence? Where is the bullet that killed Wendy, and the gun that fired it?"

"I'm betting he got rid of the actual evidence. Tackett refuses to tell me, but he probably threw the original slug away somewhere. I asked both Jim and Maribel what they did with the murder weapon. Neither of them would answer, but the forensic team went over Maribel's car with a fine-toothed comb. They determined that the silver paint on the mashed quarter panel is definitely from your truck, but more importantly, they found a 9mm Ruger under the backseat. It's at the lab now, but without the actual slug, I don't know if they can confirm it as the murder weapon. It depends on the detail of the photos they have on file."

"I don't like those kinds of loose ends. I hope they can confirm what we already know." Caitlyn hooked a loose strand of hair behind her ear. "Did you ever find out why Tackett's arm was so sore?"

Colt shrugged. "He says the pain is because of an old football injury." He closed the case folder and stood to walk around to the front of his desk. He shoved his hands in his pockets, feeling suddenly shy. "Speaking of loose ends, I was thinking, we should celebrate solving the murder. What do you think?"

"I agree. What should we do?"

He drew in a fortifying gulp of air. "Will you let me take you out for dinner tonight?" He suspended his breath and waited for her answer.

Caitlyn dropped her gaze to the floor and ran her tongue over her lip before she looked back up at him. Warmth radiated from the dark depths of her chocolate eyes. "I'd like that."

Colt worked hard at not letting his smile get too big and

goofy. "I'll pick you up at your place then, if that's all right with you?"

Caitlyn bit down on her bottom lip and her cheeks flushed a warm pink. "What time should I be ready?"

THAT EVENING CAITLYN slipped into one of the few skirts she owned. The turquoise fabric with its brown and gold design hung an inch above her knees and flared out full when she twirled. She belted a silky white blouse at her waist. Caitlyn didn't own any high heels, which was good, because she'd probably break her ankle if she tried to wear them. But she thought the skirt looked nice with her dressiest cowboy boots. She had braided her hair when it was wet, and now that it was dry, it cascaded in long luscious waves over her shoulders. Caitlyn hardly ever wore makeup, but tonight she dabbed a thin layer over the remaining greenish brown bruises on her face. She applied mascara, dusted her nose with a shimmery powder, and glossed her lips.

Caitlyn felt as though she were in high school again, the way grasshoppers were jumping around in her stomach. She laughed at herself. *It's just Colt. You've known him almost your entire life.* Still, she couldn't shake her nerves.

Smiling at herself in the mirror, Caitlyn ran her fingers over her hair. For the first time she could remember, she was filled with clarity and purpose. She'd been in her element while helping solve Wendy Gessler's murder and loved everything about the police work, including the thrill of danger. *Things are finally falling into place.*

She heard Colt's Jeep roll up the drive, and she skipped to her room to spray a whiff of perfume on her throat—the crowning touch. Renegade followed her in and sat, watching her primp.

"I hope you don't mind staying home by yourself tonight, Ren. But I don't think they let dogs into fancy restaurants. At least not off-duty K9s, anyway." She stroked his face, and he licked her hand, thumping his tail on the floor.

A knock sounded at the door. "Come on in," Caitlyn called. Colt stepped in, and blood rushed to her head. She blinked at him. He was incredibly handsome in a dark suit jacket that he wore over a light blue shirt. He'd had a fresh haircut since she saw him earlier that afternoon, too.

"Glad to see you got your window fixed," he said before their eyes met. His gaze assessed her, traveling up and down her frame, and an appreciative smile spread across his mouth.

Caitlyn swept a lock of hair behind her ear and moistened her lips. "I don't think I've ever seen you wear a tie. Very sharp."

His grin broadened. "I don't think I've ever seen you wear a dress. You're beautiful, Catie."

Pleasure spread across her skin like warm honey at his compliment. Suddenly, her arms felt gawky and awkward—she wasn't sure what to do with her hands. "Thank you." She stammered, bending to collect her purse from the couch.

"Ready to go?"

Caitlyn nodded and double-checked Renegade's food and water. She made sure he had his favorite toy to play with. "We won't be late, Ren."

Colt placed his hand on her lower back and guided her toward the door. "Is he gonna growl at me if I get you back after curfew?"

Caitlyn playfully shoved his shoulder. "Probably."

IT HAD BEEN years since Caitlyn had gone on a date, let alone been anywhere this nice for dinner. At first, she felt out of place, but after a glass of Sauvignon Blanc, she relaxed. Colt reached across the table and took her hand in his. "I'm so glad you agreed to come out with me tonight."

"Me too." Caitlyn smiled and glanced around the elegant dining room of the new golf club's restaurant. Shades of dark blue, cherry wood, and brushed nickel accents graced the rich room. They draped the dinner tables in white linen, and candles winked through decorative lanterns at their centers. Caitlyn took it all in before she returned her gaze to Colt. "Things have changed between us over the past weeks, haven't they?"

The green in his eyes darkened, and his mouth curled up on one side. He leaned forward, his tone intense. "Does that mean you've finally forgiven me?"

Caitlyn rubbed her thumb across his knuckles. "You were just a kid." She smiled playfully. "But you've grown up nicely. I forgive you for the mistakes you made after graduation, Colt." She dropped her gaze to their hands, and a gentle laugh softened her words. "Although, I'm not sure how I feel about the fact that you actually thought I could be a murderer." She widened her smile. When spoken aloud, the thought still jabbed at her heart, but she wanted to let her grudges go. "Even so, I think maybe it's time for us to move forward."

The concern in Colt's eyes softened, and the skin at their corners crinkled. "You don't know how happy that makes me." He lifted her hand to his mouth and kissed it before raising his wineglass. "Here's to our future." They tapped their glasses in cheers and sipped. "And another toast, to working together." They clinked their goblets again.

Caitlyn smiled. "That reminds me—I forgot to tell you I registered for the Law Enforcement Academy. When I graduate, in about six months, I'll be a qualified law enforcement officer, and as soon as Renegade completes his training, so will he."

"That's great, Catie. By the time I'm officially elected as Sheriff, you will both be fully qualified to be my deputies." His smile brightened the handsome face above his square jaw, and the golden flecks in his eyes glowed.

"Not so fast, Colt." She enjoyed watching the light play in his eyes and knew what she was about to say would dim it.

He raised his eyebrows in question. "Don't you want to work in Moose Creek?"

"Yes, I do. But you know we can't be anything more than friends if we work together."

As if she'd flipped a switch, the light was gone. "Then maybe you could get a job in Sundance or somewhere?"

"Don't you want to work with me?"

"Yeah, but..." he searched her eyes. "I was hoping for more."

"I don't want to move too fast. I forgive you, Colt, but I don't want to risk getting hurt again. Can't we just be friends and co-workers for a while? Take our time?"

A furrow formed between his brows, and Caitlyn hated that she put the disappointment in his eyes. "Besides, who knows? Maybe someday, I'll be the sheriff and you'll have to work in another town." She teased, hoping to brighten his mood.

He gazed at her, considering her words, then finally he gave her that deliciously wicked grin that made her want to jump in his lap. "I guess we'll just have to see."

Thank you so much for reading Renegade! I hope you love Caitlyn, Colt - and of course, Renegade as much as I do! The next book in the Tin Star K9 Series continues their story with new thrilling mysteries and adventures.

Order Maverick now!

If you enjoyed Renegade, I would be honored if you would please write a quick review.

Review Renegade

Thank you!

Book 2 in the Tin Star K9 Series

Maverick

WHEN K9 RENEGADE finds a single black high-heeled shoe with a blood-red sole, he and his handler, Deputy Caitlyn Reed search for its missing twin. They find it on the foot of a woman's body floating face down in a mountain lake.

The death appears to be a suicide, but when Deputy Reed and Sheriff Colt Branson search for the woman's identity, they come face to face with a ruthless killer.

If you like unexpected twists and nail-biting thrills, you'll love Maverick ~ Book 2 of the Tin Star K9 Series.

Get your copy!

For Free Books and to join my reader group, visit my website at Jodi-Burnett.com.

ACKNOWLEDGMENTS

In the process of writing this novel, I have learned more about Belgian Malinois, their incredible capabilities, and witnessed the intense relationship many share with their handlers. These inspiring K9 teams are what I hold in my mind's eye as I write about Renegade. We are fortunate to have such amazing and brave dogs serve our country both in the military and in police work. Their work-ethic is beyond imagining. Thanks to this incredible breed for inspiring me.

I'd like to thank my writing partner and first reader, G. K. Brady, who holds my toes to the fire and helps me put out my best work. During the development of Renegade, G. K. invited me to spend several days of intense writing time at her mountain retreat. It was a wonderful and much needed time! Thank you, G. K.! G. K. Brady writes Hockey Romance in The Playmakers Series. Find her books on Amazon.com.

As always, I must thank my husband for being my rock. His encouragement keeps me going. Thank you so much, Chris. For everything. We have a wonderful life! I love you!

ABOUT THE AUTHOR

Jodi Burnett is a Colorado native. She loves writing Mystery and Suspense Thrillers from her small ranch southeast of Denver where she also enjoys her horses, complains about her cows, and writes to create a home for her imaginings. Inspired by life in the country, Jodi fosters her creative side by writing, watercolor painting, quilting, and crafting stained-glass. She is a member of Sisters In Crime and Rocky Mountain Fiction Writers.

ALSO BY JODI BURNETT

Flint River Series

Run For The Hills

Hidden In The Hills

Danger In The Hills

FBI-K9 Thriller Series

Avenging Adam

Body Count

Concealed Cargo

Mile High Mayhem

Tin Star K9 Series

RENEGADE

MAVERICK

Made in United States
Orlando, FL
23 April 2022

17113650R00146